# INTERLUDES
## & Lunch

A collection of short stories by
# William A. Spradley

PBL Limited
Ottumwa, Iowa

*This is a work of fiction. All characters in this book have no existence outside the imagination of the author.*

10  9  8  7  6  5  4  3  2  1

ISBN: 1892689561
ISBN 13: 9781892689566

Printed in the United States of America

# DEDICATION

For Atie.
How I wish she were here for this.
How I wish she were here for everything.

# TABLE OF CONTENTS

# CADILLAC WALK

It was a quiet evening at the lobby bar of the Concord Inn. Nursing a beer and talking to Deon the bartender, I heard a clickity-click on the marble floor. Turning my head toward whoever was wearing the high heels, I gazed upon an exquisite, statuesque angel – five feet eight and a hundred and twenty-five pounds. I marveled at her fluid movement. Her wavy long hair was the color of the golden summer grass on Mt. Diablo.

As she jiggled past the bar and out the door, Deon remarked, "She gots the Cadillac walk."

"What the hell's that?"

"Man, dat means if you get involved with dat woman, you gon' buy her a Cadillac 'fore it's all over."

"No shit, I think you're right. We could probably both get arrested for what we're thinking."

"I know I would." He stole a glance around the room.

"I'm going over to the buffet. I'll see you later."

"I'll be here, Mr. B. I ain't goin' no place."

An hour later, I was back at the same stool when I heard a familiar sound. When the heel clicks silenced, I turned to my right and saw her sitting one stool away.

"Gin and tonic, Deon," she said.

"Sure thing, Miss Melissa."

Melissa swiveled my way and said, "You're new here, aren't you?"

"Yep, I got here night before last. What's a nice woman like you doing in a place like this?"

She chuckled and said, "I'm kind of hiding out."

"You work undercover?"

"Ha! You've been at this game awhile, haven't you?"

"Yeah, I travel a lot. My name's Bill, by the way."

"I'm Melissa. Originally from Beaufort, South Carolina. I had to leave; I'm kind of in witness protection. My line of work is psychiatry. I heard too much from a Mafia boss in a counseling session. I'm safe now, but the feds are still paying the bill, so I decided what the hell. I'm sure you think I work a much older profession."

We exchanged tidbits of our lives, and then she asked, "Hey, do you like country music?"

"Sure," I said. "I once met Ray Wylie Hubbard. We had it out in the men's room at Diamond Jim's in Dallas."

"You sound like my kind of guy. You want to go to Bernie's?"

Out of the corner of my eye, I could see Deon shake his head *No*.

I was bored. "Sure. Should I drive?"

"You better. I may have a little drinking problem."

Bernie's was on the outskirts of town. The parking lot was full of pickups and hot rods. Even from outdoors, the band sounded great. They were heavy on the slide steel and had a solid beat.

We strolled in and Melissa drew lots of leers from the drugstore cowboys drooling over the gold lamé dress tight around her curvaceous contours. There were cold stares of envy from most of the women. For someone in witness protection, she attracted a ton of attention. I began to wonder if her story was straight.

We found a table and turned our interest to the band. It was a typical California eclectic, grunge, country, and rock band. The lead singer and guitar was a grungy-looking white dude; the bass player was a Chinese kid in khakis and running shoes; the pedal steel was a Mexican in a cowboy hat; and the drummer was black and wearing an AC/DC tee shirt. Central California, all right – but they were good. They even played Eagles tunes.

Melissa ordered tequila sunrises and we drank and danced for an hour or so. She was a flashy dancer and kept me moving. I was barely keeping up. Men kept coming up to her asking for dances, but to my surprise she refused.

I told her, "If you want to dance with other guys, it's OK with me."

"No, I enjoy your company and I don't trust most of this bunch. They're a little creepy. Especially the gang in the back room playing pool. I hate going through the gauntlet of snooker sharks just to get to the john."

"Do you want to leave? We can find another joint better than this."

"Oh, no. I'm having a hell of a time. I like the music and the ambiance. You'll back me up if there's trouble, won't you?"

"Well yeah – but you aren't expecting problems, are you?"

"You never know in this place. I've seen some crazy shit in here. I can handle myself most of the time."

She was putting them down rapidly, two drinks to my one. It was getting late.

"I have to powder my nose." She giggled. "I'll be back in a minute." I was surprised she was still steady on her feet.

She'd been gone a few minutes when I heard a *crack,* followed by Melissa's voice. "Keep your hands to yourself, you hillbilly m – f –." Then another *crack.* "The same for you, dipshit."

I hurried back to the poolroom and saw two dudes in jeans and tee shirts draped over the pool table, a broken cue beside them. Four other guys stood along the wall with cues in hand, faces pale and jaws drooped. I've seen rabbits less frightened.

"What the hell happened, Melissa?"

"Well that one grabbed my ass when I walked by, and the other one was reaching so I cold-cocked him too."

"I'm thinking we should probably leave."

"You really think so, Bill?" She was laughing along with me. "I'd like to whack another one."

I grabbed her arm and escorted her toward the door. I

9

handed two twenties to the waitress as we passed by her and the band. The Chinese bass player gave us a thumbs-up.

On the way back to the hotel, Melissa joked about the evening and all that had happened. "Did you see the look on those red-necked mothers up against the wall? I'm pretty sure at least one of them crapped his pants. That was the most fun I've had in a month of Sundays."

"It was great." I was ready for more action. "What about tomorrow night? Is there another place like Bernie's around here?"

"Yeah, there's a joint up in Antioch. It's a carbon copy. You did okay, Bill. Most of these pansy-assed Californians are a drag." She reached over and gave me a kiss on the cheek.

"Are you really in the witness protection program?"

"Would I lie to you, bubba?"

I smiled to myself. "Melissa, have you ever owned a Cadillac?"

"Yeah. As a matter of fact, three of them. All gold. Why?"

I couldn't help but laugh out loud. "Just curious."

# THE GIRL WITH THE FARAWAY EYES

When he walked in the door of Tyler's Truck Stop in Winslow, Arizona, he saw her sitting in the corner booth staring out the window. Twenty-something, thin. Her stringy, sun-bleached hair and plaid flannel shirt over a plain white tee gave her the vacant look of a weary traveler. Her pale blue eyes attracted his attention. *Those eyes could penetrate your soul,* he thought.

"Is that your little yellow sports car out front?" she asked as he slumped into the booth next to hers.

"Yep, that's mine. It's a '78 Fiat Spider."

"Where you headed?" she asked.

"Chicago."

"Anybody with ya?"

"Nah. I'm alone."

"I'm headed that direction. Want some company?"

"I guess so." He hesitated. "The radio doesn't work. Guess we can sing our way there."

"Sweet. I won't make it, though, if I have to sing."

"That's okay. I'm sure there are other things you can do."

She moved to his booth and slid across the seat in front of him. "I need a ride to St. Louis."

"I'm heading straight through there. I'll stop tonight in Tucumcari. Does that work?"

"Yeah, sounds good." Her drab expression never changed.

Up close, her soft skin and pouty lips gave a soft, sexy look. She finished her coffee while he worked on his lunch. "My name's Misty, by the way. What's yours?" Her crystal blue eyes remained fixed on the rusty red hills in the distance.

"Wally."

11

She tossed her backpack into the short seat and climbed in beside him. They rode silently, only the throaty hum of the 1700-cc engine as background music.

"So, what brought you out this way?" he asked as they made their way through the Petrified Forest.

"I hated my life in St. Louis. I had to get away from my father. He was stifling. I have friends in L.A., so I headed there." Her voice was soft, husky, and clear.

"You were living at home?"

"Yeah, going to St. Louis U. It was boring and confining. Dad kept pushing me to get a business degree. It seemed so useless. He didn't like my boyfriend, and I felt like he didn't like me either. Not cool. It was time to get out."

"What about your mother?"

"Mom passed away when I was nine. That left just Dad and me. He never remarried. I think he should. It would be good for everyone. But he has a hard time. Her passing hit him harder than it did me."

"That's difficult. I just turned forty when Marti left me. Divorce is like a death. No clue where she is now. Last I heard, she was with some alcoholic wife beater. She preferred that kind of guy to someone like me. I didn't fit into her social life." His voice dropped lower and his eyes began to mist. "Not exciting enough for her."

"Too bad, you seem cool to me. Hard to know what goes on in someone else's mind. My boyfriend Brian was sweet at first, then we kinda wore on each other. He liked having more than one woman at a time. That sucked for me."

"That does suck. Guy sounds like a gem. That why you're headin' home?"

"Well actually...my dad has some problems. That's why I'm heading home."

*****

They pulled into the Motel Six on the outskirts of Tucumcari late in the evening. "One room or two?" he asked as he stopped the car.

"One'll do. I'm going over to the food mart to get some

longnecks and cigarettes. Want anything?"

"Cheese and crackers works for me."

When she got back to the car, he was unloading his bag and her backpack. "They only had a room with one queen size." He looked her way.

She didn't hesitate. "I'm cool with it. You aren't going to eat those crackers in bed, are ya?"

"What if I did? Would you throw me out?"

"Yeah, I would." A smile finally crossed her face.

"Rules. Everybody has rules."

"I don't like crumbs on my ass is all."

He turned to look her way as he was unlocking the door. She grinned back at him when he raised an eyebrow.

They finished the beer, and he was careful to keep the crumbs out of the bed. She headed to the shower.

Stepping out of the bathroom, wearing only a tee shirt, she asked, "Don't have no pajamas. Don't mind, do you?"

"Nah, don't own the damn things myself." He made his way to the shower.

She was a vigorous and demanding lover; her needs pushed his efforts to please. At last, he told her, "I hate to ruin the fun, but I have to drive tomorrow."

"I'll make sure you stay awake. Stop making excuses."

*****

At breakfast, Misty was quiet, staring out at the East New Mexico prairie. Wally, sleepy-eyed, downed several cups of coffee. "Misty, you worked me over last night. I'm completely broken today."

"That's good for you. You should be able to sit still and drive."

"I may have to stay over in St. Louis for a while." He gazed into those pale blue vacant eyes and sought a reaction. Finding none, he said, "Time to go."

They continued in quiet. Occasionally one of them would comment about the countryside.

"You were very good to me last night." He said it as just a

passing comment.

"It was all right. You're a very nice guy, Wally. Some woman should latch onto you."

"I don't seem to be able to find someone. No butterflies."

She turned to him, "Butterflies are overrated. Sometimes just being a nice guy is enough."

He pulled into a truck stop in Eureka, Missouri. She took out her cell phone and began talking. Wally went inside to pick up a few things.

When he strolled back to the car, she was nowhere to be found. He looked around and called her name at the restroom door with no reply. *Now where in the hell is she?* He went back to the counter and inquired of the clerk, "Hey, you didn't happen to notice the girl that was beside my car, did you?"

"You mean the skinny blonde wearing jeans?"

"Yeah."

"Oh, she climbed up in a big rig and headed west down the highway."

# DUTCH UNCLE

There was always something about happy hour at the Ramada Inn East in Williamsburg that made me want to come back day after day. That evening was no exception. When I bellied up to the bar I ordered a dollar draft and searched for a table.

She was sitting there by herself when she caught my eye. Thirtyish, light brown medium-length hair, with dark blue eyes, I thought she had that "catch-me, love-me" look. Turning toward me as I walked up to her table, and she flashed an inviting bright smile.

"Want some company?" I asked her.

To my surprise she said, "Sure, why should I drink alone? My name is Mary, by the way. Are you from this area?"

"No," I informed her. "I'm here on business. My name is Charley. What about you? Business or pleasure?"

"A little of both." She explained, "I work for a realty company in Atlanta. The owner bought a new Corvette and wants it shipped to Holland. I get to drive it to Portsmouth and put it on a ship for Rotterdam. I've been sightseeing in Williamsburg all day and came in here for a drink. Everyone says this is the place for happy hour."

"What a coincidence. I just came back from three months of work in the Netherlands. Yeah, this bar has a good reputation." This was the third day of my stay and I hadn't been disappointed yet. I asked if she would like another round and she nodded agreement.

When I returned to the table, she said to me, "I don't see a ring on your finger. Are you single?"

"Recently divorced." It was still a little hard for me to say.

"Me too," she said. "But I'm glad it's over." Her smile had

15

diminished somewhat. "Listen, I have a reservation at Christiana Campbell's this evening and it would be more enjoyable to share a table with interesting company than to eat alone."

"That sounds good to me." We talked about jobs and places we had been and people we knew until it was time to leave for the restaurant. We drove her car even though it was a short distance to the restaurant.

Our table was on the upstairs balcony. The sun was setting, creating a beautiful golden glow around the old houses. As we finished the first bottle of wine, the waiter came by for the umpteenth time, offering more – as he said – "Spoonbread, cause it sho' loves butter." The conversation remained light and humorous.

Two gin and tonics at the Ramada and wine with dinner began to affect Mary in a drowsy way. Her eyes glazed over and lost their focus. We were most of the way through the second bottle of Bordeaux. Mary looked straight into my eyes and said, "You're beautiful."

I peered into her deep blue eyes and replied, "You're drunk. But hold that thought, I have to go to the men's room." I left to go downstairs as she was ordering dessert and coffee.

It was a busy night at Campbell's and there was a wait to get into the small, cramped restroom. When I returned to the table, she was gone.

Thinking she had retired to the ladies' room, I asked the waiter if he had seen what happened to her. He informed me the lady had mentioned something about being tired of waiting and she walked out in a huff. I decided to go back downstairs to find out what happened.

I walked out onto the parking lot in time to see the Corvette pull out of its spot and sling gravel at me as this drunken woman made her escape.

"*C'est la vie*," I thought, as her taillights disappeared behind the spirea bushes. I decided to call it a night. I walked back to the Ramada in the warm fall evening breeze. I got ready for bed, grabbed the Le Carre novel I had started, and promptly fell asleep.

Awakened at three in the morning. I opened my door to find a Williamsburg police officer and the Ramada Inn house detective looking me over as if I were an ax murderer. "We'd like to talk to you about Mary Johnson," the house detective said.

"Who?" I asked, still groggy and half-asleep.

"Mary Johnson, a real estate person from Atlanta. We believe you spent some time with her this evening."

"Oh, that Mary." I tried to remain calm, but thought something terrible must have happened.

The Williamsburg cop replied, "We received a phone call from the Norfolk Police informing us some sailor reported taking this woman's car and some of her money and driving back to Norfolk. He said he left Mary in room 113 of the Ramada Inn West. She had passed out, so he took the car because he needed a ride back to the base. When we went to the Ramada Inn West, we found her there, out like a light. She woke up long enough to tell us about the sailor she met after you two had dinner together. They went to a bar, and that was the last thing she remembered. She told us the car belonged to her boss over in the Netherlands and was delivering it to Portsmouth to be shipped overseas."

At that point, the house detective noticed the KLM sticker on my briefcase lying on the credenza.

"Have you recently been to Holland?" he inquired.

My first thought was, *I'm dead meat and going to have to talk like a Dutch Uncle to get out of this one. They think we're stealing cars and shipping them to Europe. Why didn't I just have the fried chicken and a beer at the happy hour?*

"Yes, I was working over there for the Dutch Navy." I gave them a review of the evening's adventure. Halfway through, the police officer received a call on his walkie-talkie.

"Okay," he said. "We talked to her manager in Atlanta and he verified her story."

"Great," I sighed. "By the way, how did you find me here?"

The house detective said, "We found a piece of paper in

her purse with your name and room number on it. Crazy – she wound up in room number 113 at the Ramada West, the same as yours here at the Ramada East."

"Crazy is too mild for this whole evening." I was relieved. I seemed to have dodged a bullet.

The house detective warned me, "Try to stay out of trouble as long as you are here."

"Yes, sir, you can count on that." Of course, I was wrong, but that's another story.

They left and I went back to bed to get a little more sleep. At six o'clock that morning, the telephone rang. It was Mary, the runaway dinner partner.

Hi," she said tentatively. "I hate to ask, but I need help. Can you take me down to Norfolk to get my car and then to the airport?"

I hesitated. "Sure, where are you?"

"I'm at the Holiday Inn 1776. Room 125."

"Not 113?"

"What?" I had totally confused her.

"Never mind, I'll be there about six forty-five. Is that okay?"

"Yeah, that should give me enough time. I have directions on how to get to the shipping office in Portsmouth."

We put her bags in my car and we headed to Norfolk. When we got to the police station, they told us the car was in the impoundment lot. We found it and tried to open the door. "Don't you have a key?" I asked her.

"No, but I can see them on the seat of the car." I went back in the station and they handed me a tool to jimmy the door lock. Luckily, I was successful and we left for Portsmouth with her following me.

After going through a tunnel and a toll, I motioned for her to pull over. I wasn't sure of the street to turn onto from the highway. Mary took out the directions and showed them to me again.

"My tank is almost on empty and I don't have any money left." There was a trace of worry in her voice. "That guy took all

18

but a couple of dollars."

"Don't worry, there should be enough. We don't have far to go." I took off, expecting her to follow me. I was about halfway around the block when I noticed her car was no longer behind mine. I slowed down, but still didn't see her. I went on around, thinking she must have had trouble and was stopped somewhere. I drove all the way around the block and didn't find a trace of the Corvette. Three more times around, I decided she must have gone the other way to get on the highway. Pulling onto the highway, I soon arrived at the shipping office. Twenty minutes went by and she had not appeared.

That was it. Enough was enough. I took Mary's bags out of the car and carried them into the shipping office. Just as I was leaving the parking lot, the Corvette came roaring up in a cloud of dust with the horn honking and the driver frantically waving her arms for me to stop.

She jumped out of the car and said, "Oh my God, am I glad to see you!"

"What happened to you?"

"When you pulled out, it took a while to get the car going and I lost sight of you. I drove around the block at least three times and then turned the wrong direction and went back through the tunnel to Norfolk. That happened three times, too. The last time I got to the tunnel, I was out of money and the toll keeper wasn't going to let me through. He finally relented, gave me directions, and let me through without paying. The tank has been on empty for ten minutes and I didn't know what I was going to do. Boy, I am so happy you are here!"

We went into the shipping office, gave them the paper-work to ship the car, and got her bags. At last, we were on our way to the airport. We drove to departures and got the bags from the trunk. The runaway gave me a long hug and a kiss.

"Thanks, Charley, you saved my life."

"Hey, it was an adventure. Good luck."

I headed to Yorktown and the problems awaiting my solutions, which couldn't be as complicated as Mary.

# LITTLE RED CORVETTE

It was happy hour at the Ramada Inn in Williamsburg. The drinks were flowing, fried chicken was the evening's fare, and laughter filled the air. I was sitting at a long bar with a large group of people talking and enjoying the atmosphere. It had the feeling of something the Germans call *gemutlichkeit* – coziness. The conversations were full of jokes, and everyone was joining in the fun. Somehow, I was in the company of a couple of women who were unattached and looking for adventure and a good time.

The two women sitting across the table looked to be fortyish and were directing their conversation my way. The one on the left was sort of sweet looking and a bit on the timid side. Her companion on the right was highly aggressive and had the look of someone who knew how to take charge. She had coal-black hair and dark-blue eyes and told me she was in real estate. Real estate seems to be the occupation of divorced and middle-aged women who seek independence. Independent women never intimidate me. In fact, I am sure I could become a kept man.

We traded barbs and innuendo and pushed the envelope of mixed-company tête-à-tête.

The timid one started talking about country and western music and we wondered where we could go to hear some good C & W. The dark-eyed man-killer said, "I've wanted to go to this place outside of town but I don't want to go alone. My name is Jeanette, by the way." She tossed her car keys to me and commanded, "Here, I need a driver. Let's go."

What could I do? Turn down an offer like that? I probably should have, but the adventurer in me said, *"Give it a shot."*

After finishing our drinks, we made our way to the parking lot. I asked her which car was hers, and she pointed to a red Corvette convertible. I was thinking to myself that either I had hit the jackpot or they were going to find me mixed up in a tangle of shattered fiberglass the next day.

When we got to the car, she told me she had to transfer a bag of tomatoes from her car to her girlfriend's. She grabbed the bag out of the seat and as she was getting ready to put them away, the bag broke. Tomatoes rolled all over the parking lot, under cars, in the middle of the lot, everywhere. I was chasing them down and reaching underneath station wagons trying to carry several at once. At that point, my luck dipped down below the favorable mark as the hotel house detective walked up, took one look at me, and said, "What now?" We had been introduced the previous evening, and he had admonished me to refrain from further suspicious activities. Evidently looking underneath cars on my hands and knees seemed suspicious to him.

Jeanette the man-eater came to my aid by telling the detective that I was just being a gentleman and helping out a lady in distress. He shook his head and walked away. I believe he thought I had bad karma and attracted trouble. By this time I was beginning to feel the same way. We completed the transfer of the produce and I fired up the Corvette. It had been awhile since I'd driven a car like this but I conjured up my best Mario Andretti persona. I ran up the RPMs to make sure it was in top shape, then left the parking lot with squealing tires and a bit of fishtailing down York Street.

Jeanette punched my shoulder and said, "What are you trying to do, kill us? I'd like to have a car left when the evening is over."

"Sorry," I said. "I'm not used to driving a car like this." Which was only partially true. I had a turbocharged Mercury Capri at home, which was just as fast as the Corvette. Nevertheless, I figured I should have some fun while I had the chance. She gave me directions and soon we were in the woods. I didn't see any residences or even farms, and it was dark.

## William A. Spradley

Eventually we came to an old white clapboard-sided house sat up on cinder blocks with a Schlitz sign in the window. Surrounding the building were mostly pickup trucks with gun racks and semi cabs. One lonely Volkswagen Beetle sat in the back of the gravel lot. The red Corvette was a bit incongruous for the setting. I decided, *What the hell? The worst that can happen is a bunch of rednecks beat me senseless and throw me out the door.* Well, I was hoping that would be the worst.

When we entered, I discovered it was a true country bar. It had a big wooden dance floor with a little band – so little it was only one guy, a one-man band. He was playing an old Les Paul model guitar, a bracket around his neck held a harmonica, and on the floor was a bass drum and high hat cymbal he played with his feet. The only thing available at the bar was Schlitz in a can and little bags of potato chips. The black widow found a table and I went to the bar to get chips and beer. At least it was going to be a cheap evening.

She was a good dancer, except she wanted to lead all the time. I think she really was a take-charge kind of woman. We had danced four or five dances straight when some cowboy cut in. He was dressed like a cowboy but probably didn't know which end of a cow to milk. I started to head back to the table when a young, good-looking gal grabbed my arm and said, "Dance with me. My name is Kathy. What's yours?"

I told her, and we danced four dances. She had an engaging smile, dark auburn hair, almond eyes and a Rubenesque figure. We were sitting, enjoying our Schlitz and exchanging pleasantries, when the Wicked Witch of the West came by with the drugstore cowboy on her arm. It appeared I was going to have to find transportation back to the Ramada.

Kathy looked at me and said, "Don't worry. I'll get you home."

"Ah, that's a relief, because I don't even know where the hell I am. Thanks."

It was getting late and many of the patrons were growing a little loud and wobbly. There seemed to be a lot of competition for women who still had teeth, and I was afraid chaos might break out at any minute. I started looking for alternate portals of egress and noted only a front door and a back door.

About that time, a shouting match erupted between two guys and a woman. It kept getting louder, escalated into pushing and shoving, and fists started flying. Someone picked up one of the large trashcans at the end of the bar and hurled it onto the dance floor. There was now enough scrap aluminum on the floor to construct an F-14 Tomcat.

A biker dude started throwing cans in the direction of the bar. The barmaid's evasive action resembled one of those mechanical rabbits in a shooting gallery as she ran back and forth dodging flying objects while trying to call the cops. The band picked up his bass drum and guitar and headed to the back room.

The dance floor looked like a minefield and I turned toward the rear exit. I grabbed Kathy and told her we had better get out before real trouble began. We ran out the back and I asked her which vehicle belonged to her. She pointed to the little yellow Volkswagen Beetle and I couldn't help but laugh out loud.

"Are you laughing at my car?" she said. "Because if you are, you can walk home."

"No, it's not that," I told her. "I drove up here in a Corvette and now I'm leaving in a Beetle. How ironic is that?"

She rolled her eyes at me and said, "You should be so lucky."

As we were getting ready to pull out, the red Corvette shot out of the lot, slinging gravel and rocks at pickups and Peterbilts. I had made the right move and avoided being stranded. Kathy and I laughed about the crazy evening all the way back to Williamsburg. Before she dropped me off at the Ramada, she said, "Bill, I'm having a party tomorrow night. I have a friend who's a crab fisherman and he will probably bring a couple of bushels of blue crabs, and you won't have to drink Schlitz because it's BYOB. Here's my phone number. Call me when you get done with work and I'll give you directions."

I stood at the entrance to the Ramada and watched the yellow Beetle disappear down the street.

As I reflected upon how I survived the night without any damage, I thought about tomorrow and another party. *"Blue crabs, no red Corvette? I can live with that."*

## THE ILIUM PENINSULA BLUES,
### Or Why You Can't Sleep in the Hotel Anafartalar

The Hellespont is the place of heroic battles, mythical epics, and historical legends. It is the land of Helen, Paris, Achilles, and Hector. It is the beautiful blue waters of the Dardanelles, where east meets west. It is where armies have charged the beaches for over five thousand years. It is also the place of the modern day Canakkale, Turkey. I never thought I would be involved in a heroic battle of mythical proportions in this land of the Trojans. However, this became one for the history books. At the least, it should be mentioned in a few travel memoirs.

My trip started badly and got worse as time passed. My flight into Paris arrived late, so I had to take the afternoon flight into Istanbul. The drive down to Canakkale went well for a while. I stopped at Koru Dagi restaurant in the National Forest for their wonderful *doner kebap*, the Turkish version of the Greek gyro. Located halfway between Istanbul and Canakkale, the restaurant makes for a pleasant rest stop. Leaving Koru Dagi, coming up to the beginning of the Gallipoli peninsula, nighttime descended and the new Fiat sedan I rented had an engine flameout and came to a sudden stop.

So there I was on the side of the two-lane highway, with only a couple of semis rolling by. Darkness, and fifteen miles to the nearest gas station, heightened my anxiety.

While I weighed my options, a car pulled up with a middle-aged couple inside. They didn't speak one word of English, and my Turkish was limited to *hello, goodbye, please,* and *thank you.* I showed the gentleman how the engine wouldn't start. He motioned for me to get in his car, so we headed to the next gas station. On the way, there was soft-toned conversation between this gracious, kind Turk and his wife. That gave me a much warmer feeling than the hopelessness I had standing alongside the road in the dark. Visions of being skewered like a shish kebob and roasted by scimitar-wielding camel riders who terrorized the countryside left me cold.

When we reached the gas station, near Bolayir, an English-speaking mechanic thought he would be able to make a quick fix. I thanked the couple who had given me a ride and they went on their way. Sirhan, the mechanic, and I headed back to the Fiat, where he attempted to start that inanimate piece of sheet metal and leather, to no avail. Back to the station, to call the rental company. They sent a tow truck from Kesan down to the car and Sirhan drove me to meet them.

After I spent the night in Kesan, the garage had the Fiat up and running again. Everyone involved had been most gracious and helpful. I couldn't have been more pleased.

The ferryboat ride from Eceabat to Canakkle became a bit of a challenge as it had started to cloud over and rain. The blue waters of the Dardenelles turned green and choppy when the Meltami winds kicked up. We were bouncing like a cork, passengers holding onto their seats, and the snack bar was empty. After frantic maneuvering and constant course corrections, we arrived safely at the landing in Canakkale.

The Hotel Anafartalar is adjacent to the ferryboat landing so it wasn't difficult to find. As I checked in, the desk clerk asked if I would like a luxury suite. Eagerly accepting his offer, I welcomed the extra comfort. My optimism was misplaced. It was a suite, but luxury is not the word which should have been attached to the title.

My suite consisted of two rooms – a bedroom and a kitchenette/lounge area, with an apartment-sized refrigerator. There was no TV and no radio. Okay, I wouldn't understand the Turkish-language programs anyway. This would give me the opportunity to read a few books. Air conditioning wasn't one of the features of the Anafartalar. It was steam heat or open windows to control your comfort zone.

The first day went fairly well. The night was cool so there was no need to open the windows. Mother Nature took care of this evening. I would later be thankful for a night like that.

The next day was much warmer, and it was necessary to have the windows open to get that fine breeze off the Dardanelles. The breeze cooled down the room, but also allowed six squadrons of mosquitoes to make strafing runs on my body. Swatting didn't help, nor did hiding under the sheets.

These bloodthirsty annoyances were accompanied by the sounds of the street cart vendor hawking his wares to the vehicles awaiting the ferryboat. He was in the business of selling snacks, and all night long I could hear the shouts of *"Kebap, kebap."* Sleep didn't arrive until two a.m., when the ferry stopped running.

In the morning, I was able to find some insect repellant that helped stave off the Turkish Air Force... well, it slowed them down a little that night. The diesels and the ferry still made their noises and the kebap hawker still shouted his song.

On the following day, I had just settled into my easy chair to read some Ludlum when the tuning of the *kanun* or zither started. Since I'm a lover of all types of music, it was not a problem for me at first. Then the *zurna*, a reed instrument, started to tune up. Soon, the drummer, playing a *kudum,* banged his way into my solitude and it was no longer possible to concentrate on Jason Bourne. Since reading became difficult, I decided to have a drink in the hotel bar. I should've just buried my head in a pillow and toughed it out.

At the bar, I sat down at a stool, ordered an Efes beer and reached for a few peanuts that were in a bowl. A couple of the peanuts moved.

Looking again, I thought maybe my eyes were playing tricks on me and, by golly, they moved again. I said to myself, *These aren't Mexican jumping beans, so how are they moving?*

Just then the culprit revealed himself by poking his little cockroach head above the peanut pile. Evidently, this was the scout for the paratroop of cockroaches that began to leap from the light fixture onto the bar. I decided to take my beer to my room. Ignoring the band would be easier than ignoring the cockroach army.

I inquired at the desk if the band usually worked late into the night. The desk clerk was well aware of their activities. "Oh, yes, sir. They are very bad men who drink raki and gamble all night, after they finish playing their instruments." Wonderful. How to circumvent this problem wasn't immediately clear. I needed a plan.

When I got back to my room, the gambling and raki drinking were underway. I would start to drift off when someone would win a hand and the shouting commenced once again. The party broke up about two in the morning. Getting up at six-thirty in order to be at work at a decent time would be tough. Four hours of sleep a night wasn't going to do.

The next evening I inquired of the desk clerk if the band would again be in attendance in the room next door. "No, sir. They won't be back until Thursday."

This was Wednesday. Only a one-day reprieve to figure out how to get some sleep on the nights when the band showed up. I decided to fight fire with fire. But shopping for a boom box or the rough equivalent in Canakkale proved difficult. There was a music store where I found a variety of instruments for Turkish music, one of which was an almost-standard mandolin. I'd played around with a mandolin in a previous life.

Maybe, instead of fighting them, I should join them. Brilliant!

Wait. How can that help me? It probably wouldn't, but I wasn't going to sleep anyway. Therefore, maybe enough raki combined with a little fun with music would put me to sleep. I showed the desk clerk my new purchase and told him to let the derelict musicians (aren't all musicians derelicts?) know there was an available musician to add something new to the band.

Dinner was another story. While finishing my coffee, Lutfin, my waiter, stopped by to talk. We enjoyed one another's stories. He was interested in America and I in Turkey. While we were conversing, an AWOL cockroach from the previous night's invasion attempted to bridge the gap from one end of the table to the other. Lutfin was swift in dispatching the errant soldier -- adjacent to my empty plate—with a soup spoon. At least my appetite wasn't spoiled.

At nine that evening there was a knock on my door. The man standing there introduced himself as Ergan. He invited me to bring my instrument and join the musicians in their rehearsal. They didn't have a mandolin player so they were happy to see me. They used sheet music, so I didn't have to fake it too much. However, most of the music played in 10/8 time. As the evening and the raki wore on, I started having problems counting to 10.

The music sounded exotic and the band seemed to appreciate my enthusiasm, especially when it was my turn to dance. They said nothing about my talent-challenged mandolin strumming.

We quit playing about an hour past midnight and then the cards came out. By that time raki had racked my brain. I stumbled to my room and dropped onto the bed. Exhausted, I fell into a deep slumber.

Hey, maybe you *can* sleep at the Hotel Anafartalar.

# TINY BUBBLES

She was dressed in a suit and carried a briefcase. Tall, with raven hair, large dark eyes and an enchanting smile. Her face brightened each time we crossed paths. She was in the company of three well-dressed businessmen, and they appeared to be up and coming executives, in Portsmouth, England for a conference or negotiations.

Always dressed in business casual, I was on an installation job and seemed out of place. Still, she seemed overly friendly. Her smile haunted me during the workday and lapsed me into daydreams.

We seldom met in the evening. They evidently had business dinner engagements, and my group mostly hit the casual dining restaurants near the hotel and around town. This went on for the next four days, with each encounter friendlier than the last. I felt she was waiting just to catch sight of me. I, too, tried to time my trips through the lobby to get a glimpse of that wonderful smile.

When I explained this phenomenon to my partners, they dismissed my thoughts as delusional egomania. As Tim said, "Why would a classy lady want anything to do with a nerd like you?"

"Well, she might see something in me. It could happen, I'm sure." I was trying to justify my pipe dreams.

So far, it had been an uneventful trip, aside from sightseeing in southern England and Wales. Tea with scones, clotted cream and strawberry jam is nice, but it's neither intellectually stimulating nor adrenalin-pumping exciting. I could use something more, and this daydream was a welcome diversion.

Jim had even more to say. "I'll bet you ten pounds sterling she doesn't even say hello to you, let alone spend any time with you while we're here."

"Oh ye of little faith. Just what way shall we determine the terms of this bet? Must I have her bear witness or is my word proof enough?"

Jim's face broadcast confidence. "I'll take your word for it. I can always tell when you're lying. Your lips move."

"Aha, Jim, it does not bode well for you to speaketh of me in this manner, as I must put pen to your merit review. Thou might need to find comfort with the tech-writing group. Remember that at all times." I was beginning to fancy myself as a modern-day Henry VIII, after all of the castle tours and museums. Technical people sometimes need diversion to avoid becoming boring and mundane producers of paperwork.

The next workday was especially tiring and full of frustration because of shutdowns and delays due to Prince Andrew using the helicopter simulator next door to our installations. That evening when we returned to the hotel, I decided a little relaxation in the gigantic Greek classic style hot tub would revitalize my spirits.

I was enjoying the jets of water massaging my body when an apparent apparition came out of the women's dressing room wearing a black bikini – the smiling business executive. Her body was even more gorgeous than I had imagined.

Descending the steps into the pool, this beauty sat down in front of the powerful water jets directly in front of me. We were both enjoying the warm water when my gaze fixed on the voluptuous charms of her anatomy. They were being buffeted by bubbles and undulating in a most delightful way. My sensors locked on to this sight like a heat-seeking infrared missile.

I couldn't look away.

She noticed my highly-focused view and looked down to see where my attention had fallen. She looked up at me, smiled in that beautiful way of hers, laughed, and said, "Hi, I see you every day here in the hotel. Are you from this area?" She didn't seem to care about my staring at those delicious orbs. She was obviously proud of this asset.

It took a minute to compose myself. Then I replied, "I'm from St. Louis. How about you?"

"I thought you were an American. I'm from Manchester and here for a conference. What are you doing here?"

"Some equipment installations for the Royal Navy."

"You seem like a fun guy. Are you free tonight?"

I had trouble focusing on the fast-moving conversation. My fantasies of the last few nights were coming true. "I don't have any plans as yet. What about you?"

Before she had a chance to answer, Jim walked up and said, "There you are. I've been looking for you. The Captain called and wants to meet us for dinner to discuss a few things."

My heart sank and my chin slumped to my chest. Could he have shown up at a more unfortunate moment? I looked at her, she looked at me, and her smile turned into a pout. I shook my head and told her, "Sorry, duty calls. It was nice to meet you. Perhaps tomorrow?"

"I'm afraid we leave in the morning. Sorry."

Great, off to a boring dinner party with people I don't want to be with, while I miss the opportunity of a lifetime.

I was right. It was a dull evening. When we got back to the hotel, I checked to see if there were any messages and took a walk through the lounge to see if she might be there. No luck.

The next morning I hurried to the lobby to wait for my colleagues. There she was, standing at the counter. Positioning myself in her line of sight, I watched her finish checking out. Looking my way, the smiling angel grabbed her bags and walked straight towards me. Stretching up to my ear, she whispered, "Too bad. It would have been divine."

Stunned, I managed to say, "I think it would have been, too." Then all I could do was watch as she followed her three companions out the door and to their car.

## CHOCOLATE AND CHURROS

Most mornings she sat at a sidewalk table in front of Paco's Pequeño Venta, warming her hands around a cup of the thick, dark, hot chocolate that was Paco's specialty. She would've already wolfed down the churros that passed for breakfast. If she had been fortunate, she would be reading a copy of *Marie Claire* magazine. A morning ritual she followed with almost religious convictions.

That morning Stephan sat two tables away, drinking a *café con leche*, and reading the *Herald-Tribune*. It was the second straight morning he had noticed her drinking chocolate and reading a magazine.

This day, Pepita wore a purple Hello Kitty tee shirt that complemented her dark almond eyes. Stephan tried to conjure up a way to engage this petite *chica* who had captured his curiosity, but he was clueless as to a method of meeting her. Today, he was not so bold a man who might just walk up and introduce himself. Not shy, nor afraid, he was avoiding being misunderstood.

*"La cuenta, por favor,"* she said to the waiter, wanting to settle and leave.

*I have to figure out a way to talk to this woman.* His thoughts were confused, and he couldn't come to a solution to this simple problem. As she stood to leave, he noticed what he thought was an ever-so-slight glance his way. He nodded, but she walked past without acknowledging him. *Another missed opportunity!*

Pepita poured beer in the afternoon at Cervecería la Catedral on the Plaza. The clientele was a mix of tourists and locals. It had what Spaniards called *ambiente*. The floor was covered with paper napkins, sunflower seed shells, and slices of chorizo. The delightful aroma of Serrano ham, Manchego cheese, and shrimp floated out the door to invite passersby, as though calling, *"Try me."*

Stephan rounded the corner and caught a whiff of the la Catedral fragrance. He had been visiting the sights near the Plaza and it was tapas time. He walked inside and saw the girl from Paco's working behind the bar.

*"¡Hola!"* he said in his meager Spanish.

Pepita turned his way and replied, *"¿Como está? Dígame."*

*"Cerveza, por favor."*

Pepita smiled, drew a beer, and placed it in front of him. "Would you like some tapas, Señor?"

"I'm new here. What do you recommend?"

"I like the puntillitos -- calamaris. Also the tortilla and the fresh gambas are very good." She pointed out the various dishes in the counter case.

"I would like to try the puntillitos and the gambas, please. My name is Stephan."

*"Me llamo Pepita."* She looked at him with dancing eyes, then filled plates with fried baby squids and boiled shrimp.

"This is very good, Pepita. You made a *bueno* choice for me."

"Gracias, Stephan, I am glad you liked it. Are you here for holidays or work?"

"I was in Madrid for business. A customer told me I should visit Cádiz, so here I am. Do you know you have *muy bonita* eyes?"

Pepita blushed, *"Muchas gracias,* Stephan. You are very s*impatico."*

"When are you done with work?"

"Why do you ask, Señor?"

"You've been kind to me and I would like to buy you a drink. You can show me some of Cadiz. Would you like to do something like that?"

Hesitating, Pepita replied, *"Vale.* I would like."

He drank two more San Miguels and ordered ham and

cheese plates. They continued to talk and share the tapas he ordered. The sun had dropped low in the sky as they walked out of la Catedral.

They strolled the walkway along the seawall near the ancient ficus tree, while listening to the crashing waves on the rocks below. Stopping to watch the glowing sunset on the Atlantic, they discussed the composer Manual de Falla, who was born in Cádiz, and the wonderful flamenco guitarist Paco de Lucía. They discovered a mutual love of Spanish music and dancing. Sitting on a bench and enjoying the moonlight dancing off the waves, they continued to talk about their passions.

Stephan talked with her late into the night. "I have seen many women but none have had your beauty."

"I have only been here in Cadíz, but I dream of many travels. You must have met many young girls like me. I only know this place and these people."

"Yes, I've traveled all over the world and I've met many girls, but you are different. I believe I could sit here and talk all night. You are a fascinating woman."

He put his arms around her and held her tight. She reached up and kissed his check. They embraced until the moon started to hide behind the clouds. The seawall was now deserted. They were the only couple near the ficus tree.

"I want to spend the night with you, Stephan."

"I could keep you like this for eternity," he said. Like the others, she was now completely under his charms and had been swept off her feet. He had her powerless, he could do with her as he pleased.

The clouds had darkened and it was difficult to see anything at all. "I am yours," she whispered.

\*\*\*\*\*

Avianca flight 221 to Madrid filled up fast. The passengers hurried to their assigned seats. Stephan looked at his boarding pass and checked to see if he was in the right place. He lifted the overhead door and shoved his briefcase in

35

the rack. Glancing at the television screen on the bulkhead by the galley, he noticed the morning news on Antenna 3 showed a reporter standing by the seawall in Cadíz.

Video of the rocks, with the surf splashing on them in the early morning sun, repeated over and over. The flashy woman reporter described the scene and noted that the body found on the rocks had been clad only in a purple Hello Kitty tee shirt.

Stephan settled down in his window seat and picked up the *Herald-Tribune*. The flight attendant approached and said, "Welcome, Señor. Would you care for coffee or tea?"

Stephan paused, then smiled at her. "Do you have hot chocolate and churros?"

# MI CORAZON

Springtime brought the horse fair to Jerez de Frontera, Spain. I just happened to be there with some time on my hands. The job was easy, the weather delightful, and the people there love a party.

I noticed a flier in the lobby of the hotel for a tour to Jerez that included the bullfight and an evening at a *casita* on the fairgrounds. The casitas are large tents with a bar, food service, and music. There would be lots of *sevillana* dancing and girls in their beautiful *feria* dresses with frills, ruffles, and *mantillas*. It is a delight to see and be a part of one of the world's great parties. The price seemed right, and I wouldn't have to drive, so I could imbibe to my heart's content. The fair had bulls, *toreros*, parades, pretty girls in lovely costumes, caballeros sipping *fino* sherry on horseback, fresh shrimp, *tortillas*. Did I mention pretty girls, and more pretty girls?

I handed Tomás, the desk clerk, my credit card and said, "Count me in."

Sometimes in the mornings, a petite woman with dark brown hair, almond eyes, and a quick smile would be in the lobby of the Playa de La Luz, gathering the tourists together to take them to Arcos or the bodegas in Jerez.

I would nod and say *"Buenos días,"* and she'd reply, "Good morning." I suspected she had lived in an English-speaking country or was married to an American.

Our group was to meet in the lobby of the hotel at five o'clock in the afternoon, and I was there early and eager for this adventure. Talking with a group of English tourists was the tour guide from mornings in the lobby. I greeted her in my finest Spanish, *"Buenas tardes."*

37

## William A. Spradley

She laughed lightly, and said, "Good afternoon." When it appeared everyone was accounted for, she introduced herself as María. Of course, María. It was Spain, and Marías were as prevalent there as Margarets in England and Heidis in Germany.

She checked everyone on her list, and when she came to my name she said, "*Ah, Guillermo.*"

I said, "Yes." We gave each other a knowing smile.

When we got to the bullring, I asked if she was going to the fight. Shaking her head no, she said she didn't have the stomach for the blood, so it would be rest time for her. I hurried in to enjoy the *corrida*. It was a spectacle I didn't want to miss.

The bullfight used Portuguese riders who fight on horseback. Their horses are very beautiful Arabians for the most part. It's a thing of beauty to watch, because the horseman and his steed are as one entity when they work together. The rider doesn't use the reins very often and the mount responds to the pressure of the *torero*'s knees. They move instinctively. Often the horns of the bull narrowly miss their flanks. The Portuguese fighters put on a splendid show.

When the fight was over, María stood at the gate to get us on board the bus. "Did you enjoy the bloodbath?" she asked me.

"Yes, it was deliciously bloody."

"*Hombres,*" she said shaking her head. "*Yo no comprendo.*"

"Women," I said. "I don't understand them."

When we got to the *casita*, the party was already underway. Girls were dancing to *sevillana* music, drinks were flowing, laughter filled the air, and the *tapas* smelled wonderful. I grabbed a *copa de fino* and some *gambas al ajillo* and sat down at a table to watch the dancers. I hadn't been there long when María came up to me and said, "Guillermo, *baila conmigo por favor.*" She told me I must learn *sevillana* dancing and pulled me onto the dance floor.

I am not a dancer and have the grace of a donkey, so I was reluctant to try something as elegant as Spanish dancing. Maybe after several *finos*, but sober I was a disaster waiting to happen. She insisted, and I did not want to disappoint such a lovely *chica*. Chivalry had gotten me into trouble before and surely it could happen again.

We danced while Maria ordered, "Watch me, instead of your feet." Quick and strong, she had to prevent me from falling a few times. María laughed at my clumsiness and we drank *fino* while we danced. Either I became more graceful or Tío Pepe's wonderful blend of old and new wines fogged my memory, but I seemed to be flowing to the music like a flamenco dancer.

*Sevillanas* are very sensual, and sherry heightens one's awareness of the stimulating effect of dancing close and the intoxicating results of graceful Spanish femininity. I was becoming more enamored of Maria's charms as the evening passed. I thought she felt the same.

The spell would be placed on hold every now and then by her having to attend to her charges. Several of the men in the tourist group desired to learn *sevillanas* also. Eventually, she came to me and said, "Guillermo, Mrs. Pembrooke is a lonely widow and it would be nice if you would dance with her, *por favor.*"

How could I say no? María had been very good to me and spent more time with me than the rest of the group, so, I asked Mrs. Pembrooke to dance. She was a rather stiff sixtyish woman who tried her best to master the Spanish dances, and I doubted if she had danced since her wedding night. Still, she was a pleasant woman, and I had a good time.

By this time, the sherry was doing its evil work and my tongue began to loosen. When Maria came by and rescued me from the clutches of English primness, my Spanish was nearly fluent, thanks to good old Tío Pepe. I started saying things to her like, *"Ai, María, mi corazón esta roto."*— my heart was broken and I was in love.

María laughed and said, *"Tu estás borracho.* You are drunk."

"No," I told her. "You have stolen my heart. Will you marry me?"

## William A. Spradley

"*Mañana,* Guillermo."

"Good. You won't forget, will you?"

"No, Guillermo, I won't forget."

At the tipsy end of the evening, María and Mrs. Pembrooke pushed me back aboard the bus, where I slept until we arrived at the hotel. When we got off the bus, María asked if I could make it to my room. I told her she would have to put me to bed, and she giggled, "You are crazy." She gave me a hug and a kiss, pointed me in the direction of my room, and told me good night.

I languished through breakfast in the hotel restaurant until María walked in the door. She waved at me, and grabbed a *café con leche.* Sitting down at my table she said, "Good morning, Guillermo, I see you are up and moving. How is your head?"

"My head is a mess. But I had a lot of fun last night, didn't I?"

"*Si,* you had so much fun we are to get married today."

"Oh, no, what did I do?"

"You are fine. You just had too much *fino.*"

"I'm sure I had too much. I always pay for my evil ways. What did you say I did?"

"You asked me to marry you. I'd love to but I am still married – although not for long."

I saw the hurt in her eyes and I began to melt. I could tell by the look on her face she was wounded. "I'm sorry. What is wrong?"

"I'm married to an American sailor and we are in the middle of a divorce. He's going back to the States without me."

I knew what she was going through. It brought back the pain I felt when my first wife left me. I struggled to find words to console her.

I touched her hand. "It happens. It happened to me once."

"It will be a long time before I marry again. You are a fun man. Are you married?"

I told her my second wife had passed away and I was not sure what I wanted to do now. We talked about how things can

40

go wrong and that is how life goes. She went to greet the day's tour and I went to work.

We would have breakfast together most mornings for the next two weeks. If I saw her in the lobby with her tours, I would walk by and kiss her on the cheek and say, *"Ah, María, mi corazón."*

She would laugh and tell her guests, "Pay no attention to that crazy *Americano*, he is *muy loco*."

When my job ended, I left for the States.

I came back to the Playa de la Luz six months later and asked Tomás, the desk clerk, if María still gave tours. Tomás told me she had taken a job in Barcelona about three months before, to be near her family.

Bored and lonely, I missed seeing her flashing almond eyes. I missed our morning conversations. I missed her laughter. I missed María. I never danced the *sevillana* again.

*Ah, mi corazón.*

## DE PUTA MAL

She would be standing on the bridge most every afternoon as I made my way from Rota to the Caballo Blanco Hotel. She would be dressed in old, thin clothing with a well-worn sweater as her only protection from the chill.

It was January in southern Spain, and it had been an exceptionally cold and rainy winter season. She wrapped her arms around herself to ward off the cold, but I could tell she was shivering and miserable. I knew what she was doing there; everyone did. The Guardia Civil turned a blind eye to her, along with the other girls who walked along the highway trolling for a mark. The social security system in this socialist state did not provide all people with a safety net.

This particular afternoon was bitter cold with drizzling rain. Her dark hair was matted and wet, clinging to her cheeks. I thought what it would be like to have to live like this in order to survive. She could be one of my own daughters, if they had been born here and misfortune struck them.

Pulling onto the shoulder after crossing the bridge, I motioned for her to come to the car. When she opened the car door, I could see she was soaking wet all over and shaking from the cold.

"Fifty *pesetas, Senor*."

"Get in," I replied.

"*Ah, Norte Americano, no?*" I could tell she was now wishing she had asked for one hundred pesetas. "I speak *ingles*." Her face broke out into a wide smile.

"*Si, soy Americano*." I needed to let her know I was just going to help and not seek her services. "I'm staying at the Caballo Blanco, we'll go there."

"Ay, no, they do not like me there."

"I'm not going to take you to a room; we're going to the cafe-bar."

"*Vale.*"

When we walked in, the bartender motioned for her to leave.

"No, Manuel, she's with me," I told him.

He whispered in my ear, "Senor, that woman is a prostitute and you do not want anything to do with her. She is not a good woman."

"I know what she is. She's a human being, and I just want to talk to her."

Manuel gave me the usual Spanish shrug, shoulders up, palms skyward. I knew what he was thinking. Crazy *Americano.*

I might have been crazy, but she had bothered me since the first time I saw her, and I had to do something. Guilt was the driving force, I'm sure, but guilt is a good enough reason to cleanse your soul.

She sat down at a table while I asked Manuel to bring us some *tapas*, a hot chocolate, and a glass of sherry. I sat beside her.

She put a hand on my shoulder and said, "*Tu eres muy simpatico.*" She thought me sympathetic.

"What is your name?" I asked. Looking into my eyes, she hesitated.

"Consuelo. But you can call me *Pepita*. That is what *mis amigas* call me."

Trying to put her at ease, I said, "I knew a girl in Barcelona named Pepita many years ago."

I asked about her family. She told me that both her parents had died when she was very young. Her aunt and uncle took her to live in an apartment on the north side of Puerto. The apartments are built around a central fountain that's the water supply for all of the inhabitants of the community. There is only one room with a small cooking area, no windows, only a single light fixture in the middle. Sometimes as many as ten people lived in a fifteen by twenty foot space. Her life was a miserable existence, and there were no prospects for anything better.

We finished the ham and *tortilla* and I asked if she would like anything more. Pepita shook her head and continued to sip the chocolate. I asked Manuel for a coffee and the girl said she would like one too.

We drank our coffee and Pepita asked about what my life was like. I tried to explain it, but she couldn't conceive of the easy life I lived. She had no education, no job, and no idea how to get either.

My shoulders slumped, my chest heaved. Fighting back the tears, I tried to find the words to comfort her. Nothing seemed adequate to ease her pain. I looked at the thin, tattered sweater she wore, her only defense against the cold. "You don't have a jacket or a coat?"

"I had a raincoat, but it was taken by a man I was with. I don't know why he would do that. It was *mucho dinero.* Some people are *malos.*"

We finished our *café con leche* and continued to talk about her uncle and aunt who couldn't find work. She was responsible for providing food and buying the occasional propane tank for fuel to cook what she could bring home. Her uncle received one hundred pesetas a month, the equivalent of twenty-five dollars. Not enough to feed the three of them, it surely wasn't enough to buy warm clothes. Survival was the reason she stood on the bridge day after day. Her family depended on her for their lives.

A tear had formed in the corner of her eye; she leaned forward to whisper these words. "Señor, I will go to your room with you. I would like to do something for you."

The tears surprised me, as she was a very tough, young girl.

"No, not necessary, Pepita. I wouldn't feel right. And I have a wife whom I love very much and would never hurt her by being unfaithful." I shouldn't have said that, as she broke down, sobbing, her breath short and gasping.

Her crying added to the sorrow I already felt. I had penetrated her pride, and I was ashamed for breaching her inner soul. We searched each other's eyes, her pain our bond. Now the tears began to roll down my cheeks. Tightness in my chest caused me to sigh. I needed to slow things down and deflect the raw feelings tearing at the two of us.

She needed comforting. How could I console her now? Searching for something, I asked her age to take her mind off my last words.

"Eighteen," she replied.

"When did you start this?"

"I was fourteen." She turned her face away from mine, too embarrassed to tell me directly.

I pulled a one hundred peseta note out of my wallet and put it in her hand. "I want you to take this to the *mercato* and get yourself a good coat for the wind and the rain."

"*Ay, no, Señor,* that would not be right. I have not done anything for it."

"Pepita, you don't have to do anything for me. Now I think you should leave, because Manuel is getting nervous."

She got up to leave and I watched her put a few sugar packs in her pants pocket. Everything was precious to her.

"Good luck, Pepita," I told her.

She came over to me and kissed my cheek, turned and walked out the door. After a few steps, she looked back at me and waved. I waved goodbye.

Manuel breathed a sigh of relief and shook his head to indicate he was glad that this odd encounter had ended without incident.

I sat at the table until darkness shadowed the tables in the bar. Had I done the right thing? I hoped so.

My job there was finished a week later, and I saw her only one more time that week. She was standing on the bridge, wearing a new windbreaker.

## SIRTAKI FOR CIGARETTES

Tall, dark-haired, dark-eyed, pregnant, French, and maybe a little crazy, Marie was what one would call big-boned. She was a waitress at Giuseppe's Bar in Genoa, Italy, an authentic sailor hangout. For a couple of my shipmates and me, Giuseppe's was a favorite. If you brought Giuseppe a couple of packs of Marlboros, you could drink all night for nothing. Sometimes the only money I spent would be on a plate of pasta.

American cigarettes were expensive contraband in Italy at the time. You had to hide the packs in your socks when you left the ship or risk them being confiscated by Italian customs or the shore patrol. Nevertheless, they bought favors, so everyone became a smuggler in this port.

Marie always grabbed me to dance with her when Zorba the Greek came up on the jukebox. She would take my hat and wear it cocked on the side of her head as she twirled around. She loved slow dances and the sensual Greek *Sirtaki*. This crazy French woman was about five months pregnant and it showed. It didn't slow her down, because she was very energetic while she waited tables and tended the bar and, of course, moved around the dance floor.

For some reason, Marie would call me *Guglielmo*, which was the Italian form of my name. She picked it and I never questioned her why. Language was not a problem for her, but I sometimes had trouble following her mash-up of English, French, Spanish and Italian. Marie would get exasperated every time I said "What?"

She would grab my uniform jumper and say to me, "*Escuche, Guglielmo.*" Listen, William. It got my attention and I could think back to my high school Latin to figure out what

46

she said.

In between waiting tables and dancing, she would sit on the bar stool next to me and we would talk. Once I asked her who was the father of her child, and Marie looked disgusted with me, but then appeared to think about it. "*Je pense, Emilio.*"

I looked incredulously at her and said, "You think it's Emilio? You don't know?"

"*Comme si, comme ça. Il est mon bambino,* and that is all."

These talks wouldn't last long. Marie had lots of nervous energy. If she didn't have a service to tend to, she would go to the jukebox and punch up Zorba the Greek.

The *Sirtaki* is a very sensual dance. It starts slow, with arms locked on the shoulder of the person next to you. It increases gradually in tempo to a frenzied crescendo much like the Spanish Bolero.

I was not very good at this. I was not very good at any dance for that matter, and Marie would tap me on the back of the head when I missed a step. She would look at me, laugh, and say, "*Attention*" in French. I would start giggling and getting behind in the steps. That would cause her to break out in glee with her slightly gravel voice.

This went on for most of a week, and each evening would end with a very close slow dance. We were spending more time together as each day went by. I asked her what she was going to do when the baby came and she could not work for a while. Marie was ambivalent about it. "I live with *mon ami* and have enough money. I have been saving for this. I am not worried."

I only understood the nuclear family, and this would not have worked for me. However, Marie was very independent and she felt like she did not need a man to be around to help raise the child. "I would rather have no man than a bad man," she told me. "You would be a good father, *je pense*. But you won't be here, *n'est-ce pas?*"

"No," I said. "I have other commitments."

"See, that is the way always. I have only me. I will be happy, for the *bambino* will be mine and no one else's."

### William A. Spradley

I couldn't argue with her because it had nothing to do
with me. It was best that I keep my mouth shut and have fun
with her while I could. My ship would be leaving in a few days,
and I would not see her again so it was better to stay neutral.
We were dancing partners and that was all we would ever be.

A couple of days before we pulled out, the weather turned
dark and it began to rain. I felt a foreboding that made the rain
even colder. I walked into the bar and didn't see her. I asked
Giuseppe, "Where is Marie?"

"In hospital."

"What happened?"

"A problem with the bambino. It is *morto*."

The baby had died? Shocked, I could not talk for some
time. I felt terribly sad. Marie was such a happy person and
had looked forward to having this child. Now, it was gone.

I stumbled out of Giuseppe's and wandered the streets of
Genoa in the rain for some time before returning to the ship. I
hadn't known her long, but I felt like we had a kind of bond. I
didn't think something like this could punch me in the gut. She
was just a dancing partner, so why was I so concerned?

When I hear Zorba the Greek or any Sirtaki music, I
think of Marie and wonder what happened to her. I wish I
could have been there when she needed someone. Of course,
she would have been disappointed in me that I felt guilt for
something that was not my fault. She would have tapped me on
the back of the head and told me, "*Attention, Guglielmo –
escuche!*"

# TRAIN TO TOLEDO

Having flown into Madrid after a week of meetings in Lisbon, I was dog tired, so I opted for making it an early evening. Dinner in the Intercontinental Hotel dining room without the crowds of tourists gave me the quiet I sought. Sitting alone two tables away was an attractive Asian woman. Normally I would have struck up a conversation, but I needed solitude.

With nothing on my schedule for the weekend, I decided on a trip to Toledo. I had driven past that wonderful historic city a couple of times but I was never able to stop and explore.

The concierge helped me arrange a trip there for the next day. A bus tour was available, or I could simply take the train. The latter sounded good to me. He ordered tickets and told me there would be a shuttle in the morning to take a couple others and me to the station. As I turned around to leave the concierge desk, I nearly walked into her – the woman from the dining room.

She was short and well-proportioned, with coal black hair. Almond-eyed and southeastern Asian, she was dressed in a dark business suit with a white lace blouse. I excused myself and she said, "I too want to see Toledo tomorrow. Have you been there before?"

"No, only in passing through on the highway."

"Maybe we can see it together."

Though I wasn't sure how I felt about companionship, there was no need for both of us to spend the day alone. She appeared quiet, well-mannered, and well-educated, but also a bit sorrowful and reflective.

"Sure," I said. "If you would like company, we could travel together."

She smiled. "That would be great. My name is Angelina."

"I'm Dave. We can meet here in the lobby tomorrow morning. Have a good evening."

Before turning in for the night, I started to think about this woman and what might be her circumstances. Either she was lonely enough to want to spend the day with a stranger, or there was something else behind her eagerness. She seemed to be carrying a great weight and I suspected her situation might be the same as my own.

The next morning I was sitting in the dining room, reading the *Herald Tribune* and finishing my *café con leche,* when she walked up to my table and said, "Good morning, Dave. May I sit with you?"

"Of course. Good morning to you, Angelina. Did you sleep well?"

"Not so good. Still having jet lag because of the trip from Manila."

"Oh, that is a long trip. How many hours?"

"Over twenty, with two stops on the way. It's very tiring. I arrived here Thursday and nearly slept the clock around." The waiter came by and she ordered coffee and toast with a boiled egg. "You can read your paper, I don't mind. My husband used to read the morning paper, so I am used to it."

I liked her attitude. "Sometimes women believe it's a way to avoid conversations, but in reality men are the same all over. They just like to read the paper. I don't know why, but it's a universal male ritual."

Angelina added, "Some women believe a man should give a hundred percent attention to them. I don't think that is possible, or healthy. Everyone needs their space and some solitude."

"You're a perceptive woman. Your husband is a lucky man." Would this prompt her to open up about her status?

"We were lucky to have each other. He died of a heart attack a year ago. He was a good man."

"What a coincidence. My wife passed away of cancer recently. We have both had a difficult time. Oh, I see it's nearly eight-thirty. We need to catch our shuttle."

It was a short train ride from Madrid to Toledo. We sat across from one another and talked about our homes.

"I have never been to America. Have you been to the Philippines?"

"I've been in Manila once for just a day, but I have been to Olongapo, where the big navy base is located, several times."

"Oh you were in the Navy then?" She smiled. Olongapo was a wild and crazy town while I was there. It had a dubious reputation. Bars, B-girls, rock bands and bedlam were the norm during its military heyday. Most sailors remembered it fondly as a fun liberty port; most Filipinos thought of it as a sin city disgrace.

"Yes, back in the sixties. It was a very different time. I was much younger and very foolish in those days."

Her eyes brightened and a smile crossed her face. "I lived in Olongapo during that time. I was a singer in a band that played in the clubs on Magsaysay Boulevard."

"Are you serious? We might have seen one another. I can't believe it." Many things came to mind from a long time ago and so far away.

"My husband was the lead guitarist. We worked in the Go-Go Club and also the Anchor Club in Caviti City for several years. When the war ended, we moved back to Manila. We earned enough money to buy our own restaurant and sold it when my husband's health started to deteriorate. I went to work for a large accounting firm to supplement our income. "

"My goodness, I remember the Go-Go Club. My friend Martin and I would sometimes play during the break for the band. His guitar was similar to the style of Chet Atkins and I accompanied him on the drums. It was a fun place and the band was gracious enough to let us play their instruments. Probably your husband let us play. I can't believe that we have crossed paths again after all of this time has gone by."

"Do you believe in fate, Dave?" She appeared very excited; this discovery had brought her out of the sadness that seemed to envelop her.

51

"Yes, I do. It has happened to me many times." Meeting someone from long ago made the world smaller and more personal.

"I believe we were supposed to meet." Angelina's face brightened and her eyes misted over.

When the train arrived at Toledo, we visited the Alcazar first. A long walk around the old fortress, enjoying the history of that storied edifice, gave us time to talk of our mutual love of history and ancient struggles. From the Moors to the Spanish Civil War, the Alcazar had a multitude of tales.

Strolling through the El Greco museum with its gaunt figures provided a visual feast that left us wondering about the artist's reasons for elongating the figures in his paintings.

"Are you as hungry as I am?" I said. We decided to take a break and have lunch in the Zocodover Square. The local delicacy is roast suckling pig, but we opted for the grilled fish along with a bottle of Diamante.

During lunch we reminisced about Olongapo and the wild times there.

"The Go-Go Club was a crazy place," I recalled. "Some of the girls working in there were so much fun. I remember they would tell you not to 'butterfly.' They would get angry if you went from place to place. One guy in my bunch had been hanging around this gal in that club and she found out he was all over town."

Angelina laughed, "I'm sure she worked him over."

"Oh yeah, she had told him she'd cut his throat if he played around. We came in one night and she was over at the bar when she saw him and wagged a finger. He told us 'Oh, no, she's going to kill me.' He didn't see her come up behind and run an ice cube across his neck. He jumped up looking for blood, and we all laughed and so did she. He thought he was a goner. I wish I had a picture of his face."

"Oh, those were such fun days." Angelina giggled.

We left the square and wandered around the shops which sold swords and other crafted metal trinkets from the foundries of Toledo, then strolled through the cathedral and admired more El Greco until we had our fill. Then we walked back down from the citadel towards the city gates and on to the train station.

On the train she remarked, "They must have used the rack on all of El Greco's people."

"Either that or there was a famine. Too bad he's not still around. His portrait of me would take off twenty pounds."

The conversation remained light all the way back to Madrid.

When we arrived at the hotel, I asked, "There's a very nice little restaurant close by. Would you be interested?"

"Thank you, I would like that."

Dinner was pleasant and intimate. We were able to laugh about the day, and pass jokes back and forth between ourselves and the waiter. We stayed there at the table drinking more of that delightful Diamante wine and lingered over *cafe espresso* and Ponche brandy.

We returned to the Intercontinental and I walked her to her room. At the door, Angelina turned to me and said, "I don't want to sleep alone tonight." She opened the door and we entered together. It felt like the natural thing to do.

The next day we visited the Prado and the Plaza Mayor. It was again a pleasant day spent talking and enjoying the ambiance of Spain. We knew our time together would be over the following day, because I had meetings to attend in Madrid and she had the conference to take up her time. Then I would leave for Seville.

At breakfast the last morning we sat quietly looking into each other's faces.

"Dave, I have laughed more the last two days than I have in a year. I will miss your funny ways."

"Aw, Angelina, you've been a delight. I think we both needed this time and fate put us together. I'll miss your laughter and smiling face."

We had been like two ships in the night that sail the same course for a while, then travel on to different ports.

## Purgatory Can Wait

"I'd go to hell with you, Rita," he slurred into his beer.

"Now that's a load of crap, Donny. You won't even take me to a movie. You're drunk again." Rita leaned over the bar. "All we ever do is hang out here at Mo's. You're the cheapest dude in Durango. And who wants to ride around in a beat-up orange and black '72 El Camino?"

"Aw, Rita. You know if I could, I would buy you nice things and take you places. It's hard to find a job around here. You know I love ya."

"God, Donny, just get the car and let's get out of this joint. I worked a double today. It would be nice if you at least worked one shift."

They drove in silence on the way to her apartment. When he pulled up front, she let it all out.

"Donny, I'm sick and tired of your funky-ass car, your non-existent job, and your doublewide. Do something about it."

"But, Rita..."

"No buts, Donny. Just do it." She hurried out of the El Camino and ran up the steps, not saying another word.

When Donny got to the trailer park, he called his buddy Tim Dalton. "Tim, I need some help, man."

"I'll bring a six-pack," Tim replied.

At the kitchen table in Donny's doublewide, they brainstormed the problem – as much as they were able to brainstorm anything.

"The only solution I see is to rob a bank," Tim said, deadpan.

"Man, that's dangerous," Donny whined. "And you could go to hell for robbing a bank."

54

## Interludes & Lunch

"I don't think so, Donny. I was raised a Catholic. I think if it's not a mortal sin, you only go to Purgatory."

"You mean the ski resort or the creek?" Donny's knowledge of religion was limited to Heaven and Hell.

"God, no, Donny, you heathen. Purgatory is kinda like a holding pen. If your sins aren't too bad, you get a chance to work off the bad things you did and then you can go to Heaven. It's like probation."

"Man, I don't know. It sounds iffy to me. What about robbing a train?"

"A train? What the hell kind of train would you rob?" Tim asked.

"The Durango-Silverton steam train. This time of year, it's full of rich tourists. We could get rings, watches, wallets, and ladies' jewelry. There's no security like in a bank."

"You know, Donny, that just might work. We can use my four-wheeler to make our getaway. We'll drop a log across the tracks and when the train stops to clear it, we board and go up and down the aisles collecting the loot. It'll be easy. They'll think it's part of the attraction. We get back on the four-wheeler and run back to town. Hell, yes, this'll work."

The next morning Donny called Rita with his exciting news. "Guess what, Rita? It won't be long before we have plenty of money. We'll head to Florida and live on the beach. You'll have so much gold and so many diamonds you can wear new ones every day."

"Donny, are you crazy? Whatcha gonna do? Rob a bank?"

"Hell, no, Rita. I have a plan. You'll see."

"I'm not gonna hold my breath."

Donny and Tim started scouting out places that would work for their daring plan. They decided the curve right before the train entered the Purgatory Creek trestle would be the best spot. The trail running up the canyon came close to the tracks and the train would have to slow down for the curve. They notched a tree to make it a quick drop across the tracks. They had covered everything, or so they thought.

That Wednesday morning was sunny and clear. Donny

55

and Tim dropped the spruce tree across the narrow gauge tracks just short of the trestle. They sat behind the downed tree waiting for the sound of a steam engine.

"I feel like Jerry Jeff," said Donny.

"Yeah, like *Desperados Waiting for a Train*. This will be really cool."

"I sure hope we don't have to shoot anyone," Donny squeaked.

"Aw, it's just tourists. They ain't gonna be no cops on that train. No one would ever think of robbing a tourist train. That's why this is such a brilliant idea."

Off in the distance came the sound of a steam whistle.

"It's show time, Tim."

They slipped on their ski masks and pulled out the handguns.

Donny fussed with the mask. "This damned thing is itchy in the summer."

"It won't take long. We'll be outta here in no time."

As the train rounded the bend, the engineer spotted the tree across the tracks and slammed on the brakes. The big wheels squealed and sparks flew from the rails. The engine stopped a yard from the log.

They leaped over the tree, Tim climbing up into the first passenger car and Donny into the second.

Donny stood at the end of the aisle and shouted, "This here is a robbery. Everyone just keep calm and no one will get hurt. When I walk down the aisle, put your loot in this backpack. We need watches, rings, wallets, and any kind of jewelry. So don't nobody cause any trouble and you'll be okay."

He started down between the seats, holding open the backpack and pointing to items he wanted the riders to surrender. Some passengers smiled, thinking it was part of a show. A taste of the Old West.

At the fourth seat in sat Mable McPherson, retired school teacher from Ottumwa, Iowa, with her husband Jack, a former farm implement salesman. "Oh, this is just so neat. A train robbery! Wait till I tell Ethel. She'll be so jealous." She looked up at Donny. "We'll get our stuff back, won't we? How'll we do that? Do you hold it till we get to Silverton or what?"

Donny growled at her, "Lady, just hand over the stuff." He looked over at Jack and asked, "Doesn't this woman ever shut up?"

Jack shook his head, "Nah, I've been trying for forty-two years. Good luck."

Donny walked on, shaking his head at the woman's noise. She continued on, "How neat."

Further down the car, Frank Jessop, retired carpenter and member of the U.S. Marshalls Auxiliary from El Dorado, Kansas, brought his six-foot three-inch frame to a standing position. Dressed in a ten-gallon Stetson, western-cut coat with a bolo tie and cowboy boots as accessories, he cut a handsome figure. He drew a snub-nosed .38 from his coat pocket and pointed it toward Donny. "Hold it right there, Mister. Drop that gun and turn around."

"Who the hell are you?" Donny asked.

"I'm a U.S. Marshall and you're under arrest."

Mable squealed with delight.

The mask was bothering Donny so he raised his .22 pistol to scratch his head. When he did, Frank pulled back the hammer on the .38. It was Randolph Scott and Lash Larue transported to the high-tech cell phone age.

Donny started to bring the gun down and Frank squeezed off two rounds in rapid succession, hitting Donny in the chest.

Hearing the shots, Tim rushed to Donny's car and spotted him lying on the floor. He picked Donny's head up and cried, "God, Donny you're hit. You gonna be okay?"

As he slowly drifted away to that great holding pen in the sky, Donny looked up at Tim and whispered, "I'm a goner, Tim. Tell Rita I'll be waitin' for her in Purgatory."

*William A. Spradley*

# A WING AND A PRAYER

Her name was Norma Jean. Fiftyish, well-preserved, divorced, beautiful, and a darn good singer, she was vivacious and a ton of fun.

His name was Johnny. Seventyish, worn out, divorced and widowed, and slightly crazy, he was a late blooming novelist and short story writer.

Together a most unlikely couple... Actually not a couple. More a couple of buddies. She liked to party and he liked to watch her back. He was very protective of her.

They met during a trivia and karaoke night at a local pub. Introduced by a mutual friend, sardonic banter between them came naturally. Theirs could never be a serious romantic relationship, but each enjoyed the other's sense of humor, and both loved a good time. Although a million miles apart in backgrounds, they shared a love of music.

At Panama Joe's one night she announced, "The emcee talked me into entering a karaoke contest at The Blue Lagoon. Will you back me up?"

He wondered at this. "What do you mean, 'back me up?' Do you mean sing back up? Keep the cops off your tail? Chip in financial support or play bodyguard?"

"No, ya dork, I can't drink and drive, and I can't sing without drinkin', so I need you to transport me to and from."

"Are there benefits to this arrangement?"

"Yeah, Johnny boy, you get to listen to me sing." Her eyes sparkled and her grin widened when she worked on him like this. He was a sucker for a pretty face.

He pretended to balk. "Why do I do this stuff? I should be in the Caribbean fishin' the Pylons."

"Here's a big, wet, sloppy kiss for you, sugar."

"Oh Lord, I am such a schmuck."

"You love it, you know you do."

Shaking his head he asked, "What time, baby cakes?"

"8:12-ish."

"Not 8:10 or 8:15, 8:12-ish?"

She pointed her finger, mocking. "That's right, honey, be on the money."

He arrived at 8:00 and she was finishing her hair. At 8:12, she turned to him and said, "Okay, I'm ready. I need a drink. I'm so nervous, I've had a vodka and Red Bull already. Let's hit it."

At the Blue Lagoon, the drones surrounded the queen bee as soon as she sat down. Johnny shook his head and laughed as they each tried to elbow into position to get close to Norma Jean. It was like flies to honey.

Her turn to sing was near the end of the group. She downed two more vodka and Red Bulls before heading to the stage. "Johnny, my tummy aches, I'm so scared."

"Norma Jean, you'll do a great job. You always do. Relax, we're all pulling for you."

The singing went well. The judges had great things to say about her performance.

Still, she appeared dissatisfied. Johnny gave her a squeeze when she returned to the table. The next song met with even more approval, even though she had stumbled over the lyrics. She had the crowd on her side with that bubbling personality. Watching her was like having champagne flowing in your veins.

The combination of vodka and Red Bull had a devastating effect. The Red Bull made her hyperactive, the vodka made her loud and crazy. Together they created a roller coaster emotional state. After the competition, Norma Jean had another drink. A couple of guys began to press her hard to go somewhere else with them. She gave Johnny a hopeful look. It was time to make their exit.

"Are you ready, sweet thing?" Johnny tried to herd her

out of the door.

"I'm ready, Sunshine." He made sure she got into the car and home safely.

What started out as once or twice a week soon turned into three or four nights a week. The drinking became heavier and the mood swings more pronounced. In Panama Joe's one evening, a friend of Norma Jean's came to their table and started a deep conversation with Johnny. They shared a mutual interest in poetry and travel. Her name was Linda and she had had a few too many glasses of wine. She took Johnny by the hand and out to the dance floor. They swayed closely to slow dancing numbers and exchanged soft kisses. Norma Jean's eyes followed their every move.

When Linda retreated to the powder room, Norma Jean let loose a string of accusations. "You had your hand on her ass, Johnny. You're a damn hooker."

"What if I did? Why should you care? You always have your pretty boys to dance with. What's the difference?"

"Because."

"Because what?"

She was slow to answer, "Just because, dammit."

He squinted at her and tried to figure out what was happening. She had said many times they were just casual friends, so she should have been happy he was having fun. Norma Jean seldom danced with him, so he puzzled over her reaction.

As they prepared to leave, Norma said, "Holy crap! Al's coming in the door. Honey, we need to get out of here before he sees me."

"Who's Al?"

"We used to date. He's a cop, very jealous, and thinks I still belong to him. He's creepy and has a nasty streak."

"Come on, we'll escape out the back."

"Thanks, Johnny boy. You're a good wingman."

They were going out more and staying later as time went by. It was now four or five times a week and beginning to wear on him. They were drinking more and laughing less.

## Interludes & Lunch

At the Blue Note one night, Johnny pleaded, "Norma, we need to slow down a little. This pace is killing me."

"Well, Johnny, if you're not up to it, maybe I need a new wingman."

"That's not fair. You shouldn't treat me that way."

"Aw, Johnny, let's have one more and head home."

A tall burly man with a mean disposition started putting the rush on Norma. Al had caught up to them.

"Come on, babe, let's dance," Al said. "You've been hiding from me. You shouldn't do that."

"Nah, Al, I'm kinda tired. How about a rain check?"

"Look. I ain't got all night."

Johnny stepped in to ease them apart. "Buddy, she said no, so let it be."

"Who the hell are you, old man?"

"I'm a friend of hers and you need to take it easy."

"She's my squeeze and she's goin' home with me. Get out of the way."

Norma shouted, "Al, dammit! I don't belong to anybody. Johnny's just lookin' out for me."

Johnny put his arms out to keep her behind him. "We don't want any trouble. Just let us by. We haven't harmed you in any way."

Al pulled his service revolver from its holster behind his back. "Back off. This is between her and me."

"Easy, man, there's no need for that."

Al raised the gun to chest level and eased off the safety. Norma stepped in front of Johnny and grabbed the gun. The bullet went through her chest and on through Johnny's, breaking a glass of tequila on the bar. They fell to the floor in a crash of chairs and beer bottles.

Sprawled out amidst broken chairs, Johnny reached over to take her hand and whispered, "Love ya, Norma Jean."

She squeezed his hand and said, "I love you too," as their lives flowed away on the barroom floor.

*William A. Spradley*

## It's Not Love, But It's Not Bad

April in Paris. If it was a dry day, he would take his lunch on a sidewalk table at La Petite Zinc in St. Germain. His laptop was a constant companion. Sometimes he drank St. Emilion reds and sometimes Rhône whites; it depended on Chef Antoine's catch of the day. If the fish wasn't to his standard, he would have the entrecôte and the red. He was finicky that way.

As he took the first bite of his salad, she asked, "Mind if I share your table?"

"You don't have any disagreeable habits, do you? Like falling for older men?" he asked with a straight face.

Startled, then laughing, she said, "No, I try to avoid it."

"Good. Please sit down."

"Thank you. I'll try to practice my self-discipline. We haven't been properly introduced. I'm Fiona."

"I'm sorry, but I enjoy teasing attractive young women. I'm such an overbearing ass at times. My name is Frank."

"No need to apologize. We English have learned to tolerate bluntness from the Colonies."

"God bless the Queen. Are you visiting?"

"No, I'm a student."

"Sorbonne?"

"Yes, I'm studying languages, majoring in French, Russian, and also Mandarin. Do you live here?"

"I have an apartment down the street. I hang out in this area trying to channel Hemingway and Fitzgerald. I write romance novels. It pays the bills."

Fiona looked surprised. "Romance novels? You don't seem the type."

"I have my moments. Care to find out?"

"Sorry; no, thank you. I'm English you know."

"Smoldering passion, I'm thinking." He pressed. "A dormant volcano about to erupt?"

"Go back to your book."

She ordered. He typed. She observed as he stabbed the entrecôte in between writing paragraphs. Frank had manufactured so many stories that the words flowed easily.

"Is there a formula for these things you write?"

"Things? You call this 'blood, sweat, and tears,' *things*? I pour my heart and soul into these stories. I work as hard at writing as you do at studying. Or are you just a society girl financed by Daddy? I took you for a commoner."

Fiona's jaw tightened. Her dark eyes flashing, she exploded. "You cheeky bastard! My father owned a souvenir shop in Lyme Regis. I had a public school education and worked hard to get a fellowship to the Sorbonne."

"Ah, were you the French Lieutenant's woman?"

She gave him a cold stare, and then slowly a smile overtook the anger. "You really are a piece of work, aren't you?"

A broad grin spread across his face. "I jacked you up quickly, eh? It's the business. Makes me a sarcastic jerk. You should have slapped me and gone elsewhere."

"For some insane reason, I am enjoying your madness. It's sexy in a perverse way. However, don't get your hopes up. My assessment isn't final."

"I can wait."

Enjoying the last few bites of the crab salad, Fiona sat mesmerized watching Frank's fingers fly over the keyboard. He rarely stopped to think. Words flowed like water in a mountain stream.

"So, do you have one of these literary masterpieces with you?"

He reached into his bag and handed a book to her. "Here."

"My God, who is this hunk of a man on the cover?"

"He's a pig farmer from Unadilla, Nebraska."

"Amazing. Do you sit here all day?"

"Occasionally, I entice some sweet young thing to my

apartment for a spot of heavy breathing. Generally, I leave here at four and retreat to my desk."

"Do you have claret at your place?"

He raised an eyebrow. "Racks of it. I even have food there and some bloody tea."

\*\*\*\*\*

The rain began at six o'clock, drumming a dancing song on the bedroom window. They were wrapped around one another, exhausted. Her raven hair lay in contrast against his white skin.

"I'm famished. Where is that bloody tea?"

He rolled over on his side. "Must I do everything? You made me work very hard this afternoon."

She lay back on the pillow. "It's good exercise for the elderly."

"You could kill an old man this way, you know. Will a cheese omelet and sautéed mushrooms be enough for your bleedin' tea?"

\*\*\*\*\*

They met three or four times a week with the same result. On Sundays, if they both had free time, they would visit the Louvre or the Musée d'Orsay. A love of impressionists, particularly Monet, appealed to both.

One Sunday in May, Fiona packed a picnic lunch and they drove to Giverny in Frank's MG TD. Marveling in the beauty of Monet's dreamlike garden, they passed the afternoon talking of the changes of light and color that must have inspired the many paintings of this garden produced by the master's brushstrokes.

A park nearby became their picnic spot. He spread a blanket under a linden tree with a view of the countryside. Wine, cheese, and quiet conversation made an idyllic day complete.

Lying next to each other as the light faded, she said, "You surprise me, Frank. When I first met you, I thought you were an insensitive bore. There's a soft underbelly to you I would not have believed existed."

Frank raised up on an elbow, kissed her forehead, and whispered, "You won't give me away, will you?"

"Your secret is safe with me. No one would believe me if I told them you were a pussycat after all."

*****

Over coffee at Les Deux Magots the second Saturday in June, he asked if she had the following weekend free.

"Yes, I have some time. Why?"

"I'm thinking a trip to Épernay with wine tasting and country dining is in order. There is a very nice B&B there I would like to try."

She scrutinized his face for a trace of emotion before she spoke. "That sounds a bit romantic, Frank. What's the occasion?"

He didn't reveal his emotional state. "No occasion. It's something I think we would both enjoy. Don't try to read anything into it."

"I know we'd both enjoy it, but it still seems like a prelude to something."

He became defensive. "Why can't we have a good time and not worry about how it appears?"

"Frank, I'm always amazed by your logic. Fuzzy though it is, it's always your logic and no one else's. I'll go and we'll have a good time, but don't expect anything more than platonic platitudes from me. I'm not sure of your intentions. However, I do know I'm not ready for a love affair. I like our relationship the way it is."

"So do I. I'm not trying to maneuver you into anything. It will be a pleasant trip. We'll get out of the city for a while. I think it'll be good for us."

*****

The drive to Épernay was breathtaking. Fields of yellow sunflowers that were starting to bloom and the dark green of the vineyards provided a vivid *plein air* dreamscape. Using back roads, they crossed the Marne several times, and enjoyed the meandering, peaceful river.

The bed & breakfast Les Bischottes was quaint and friendly. When they were shown the room, they looked at one another and laughed. It was a newlywed's fantasy, including a canopy bed.

Fiona shook her head at Frank and said, "You know you don't have to do this to get in my knickers, don't you? It's established that I'm a pushover for you."

"I told you, I have no romantic notions. But it is a fantastic room, isn't it?"

The day was spent traveling from one vineyard to another. They tasted the barrels and barrels of bubbly and talked about the countryside. Dinner was an epicurean delight of quail and lamb with fresh vegetables from a local garden.

They retired to their room light-headed from endless glasses of champagne, which even three cups of coffee and fruit pastry couldn't drive away. That night Frank was very attentive and tender.

The drive back Sunday afternoon was quiet with many loving glances passing between them. "Frank, you're not getting serious about our relationship, are you?"

"What a strange thing to ask me – Frank Howard, boy Casanova. I told you, I don't do 'close.' You once called me a gigolo, remember? Let's leave it that way."

*****

July was a very busy month for both of them, Fiona with exams and Frank with a deadline. They got together occasionally until August, when she traveled back to Lyme Regis for her break.

*****

She returned the first of September for the start of classes. They met for lunch upon her return.

"I actually missed you," he told her while sipping his wine.

"Really? I didn't think that was part of your persona, Love."

"Hard to imagine that I have a soul?"

"No. That you would care for anyone but yourself is more like it."

"I was in love once, you know."

"What was she like?"

"Young. Pretty. Intelligent. Cynical. Much like you."

"You could fall in love with someone like me? I don't believe it."

"It's true."

"So what happened to this extraordinary woman?"

"She left me for a younger man. It still hurts and it's why I keep my distance now."

"Frank Howard has a heart. Who would have thought?"

"Miracles happen all the time."

*****

In early October they met at the restaurant. Her conversation was limited and the bite gone from their exchanges. He could tell she had something on her mind. "So, what's the problem?"

"There's a guy in one of my classes and we seem to be attracted to one another."

"Is it serious?"

"It could be."

"What's he like?"

"Young. Handsome. Intelligent. Rich. French. And he has the body of a pig farmer."

"I can't compete with that. My body's more like the pig than the farmer."

"We have a weeklong break coming and he's asked me to go with him to his parent's villa in Antibes. I've decided to go."

"I can't stop you."

"You know, Frank, what we had wasn't love, but it wasn't bad either."

*****

### William A. Spradley

The trip to Antibes wasn't up to her expectations. Anton was spoiled and his parents were over-indulgent. She decided she had made a mistake. Frank's maturity and biting sarcasm were more to her liking.

Upon returning from the trip to Antibes, Fiona stopped by Le Petite Zinc to talk to Frank. When she couldn't find him she inquired of the waiter, "Has Frank been here today?"

"Oh, you haven't heard? Monsieur Frank was run over by a taxi last week by the front of Les Deux Magots. It was raining and the car couldn't stop."

She gasped. Tears began to fall. "Oh my God!"

The waiter explained, "Some say he looked straight at the cab and stepped into the street."

## AGAINST THE WIND

At the memorial service, a flood of memories rushed toward me, as her sister handed me the black and white photos Janet Mae had kept close all those years. The photos filled me with so many emotions at once; I had difficulty sorting them out.

We had been sweethearts from the summer after sophomore year until the start of our senior year of high school. That year and a half provided a plethora of experiences and emotional roller coaster rides.

I moved to Seward in the spring of 1956. I first noticed her the day classes began in my new school. Not much happened between us until school ended for the summer. Then we met one afternoon at the swimming pool.

After splashing and dunking one another most of the afternoon, I asked, "Want a hot dog and a Coke?"

"Can you handle all that?"

"Sure. I tell you to get your money and go to the concession stand and buy it. Does that work?"

"You win. I want mustard on mine."

We sat on a bench by the pool and finished our snack.

"Go with me to Diane's house," she said.

I walked with her to a friend's place where we spent the rest of the afternoon talking and teasing.

*Blackboard Jungle* had made the rounds of the theatres, and since I came from the big city of Lincoln, I was a gangster. "Hood" was my new nickname. Branded a rebel, I dressed differently and listened to rock and roll, jazz, and classical music. It seemed a strange combination to most of the kids in this small rural community.

## William A. Spradley

Janet had an outspoken attitude and love of fine arts, which set her apart from most of the class. We naturally gravitated to one another. An accomplished piano player, she also played the bass clarinet in the band.

One evening I asked, "Have you read *For Whom the Bell Tolls?*"

"I love it. It broke my heart. The movie is at the Rialto. We could watch it together."

After the movie, we sat on the benches at the band shell across the street from her house. Holding one another, I asked, "Do you want to be a writer or a musician?"

"It's a hard choice. You know how I love music."

Our passion for music, writing, and each other burned hot. We had to pry ourselves apart to avoid the wrath of her father.

In the summer, I worked in the fields detasseling seed corn, and we would go to the pool in the evening. The long walk back to her house gave us plenty of time to talk. Mostly, it was only the two of us. We seldom went anywhere with anyone else.

After work, I hung out around her house and became acquainted with the family. It was a funhouse there. You never knew what would happen.

One day when I was there, the four-year-old little brother wrapped his arms around my leg and bit my ankle.

She shouted, "Jimmie, are you crazy?" I laughed at him.

During the summer, I picked up a couple of friends while working in the cornfields. Chuck, Tom, and I liked cars, electronics, and music. We did many crazy things which in this day might be called criminal. We were just having fun in a small town.

Tom had an old '37 Ford sedan. That car was both cool and a nightmare. Due to it having mechanical brakes, it often was a little cranky about stopping. It had a top made of oilcloth, chicken wire, and wooden slats. However, the best things about it were the running boards.

One night I borrowed my dad's old single-shot 12-gauge and the three of us went on a waste can hunt. It was the night

70

before trash pick-up day and we made the rounds with Tom driving, Chuck in the suicide seat, and me out on the running board. Chuck held onto my belt and fed me ammunition, while I laid the shotgun on the top of the Ford. There were a lot of blasted trash cans around town the next morning.

You have to find your own form of entertainment in the country.

Things were going swimmingly until that fateful Saturday after Thanksgiving. Tom and Chuck had come by to go for a ride. We dropped by Janet's house.

"Want to go for a ride? It's a really great day for it."

"You're not driving, are you?"

"No, Tom is. C'mon, we'll have fun."

"With you three together?"

We were cruising around the countryside enjoying the pleasant fall weather, when Tom came off a narrow bridge too fast. The right front tire hit a gravel pile and twisted the car to the right. The rapid movement caused it to turn over. In all, the police figured we rolled at least three times. All of us went through the top at the apex of the first roll, and the centrifugal force sent us flying. I only recollect looking down and seeing the roof.

I remember stumbling around in the middle of the gravel road in stocking feet, not remembering who or where I was. Sirens sounded in the distance.

A body lay on the road, crumpled, not moving.

In the hospital, Dr. Hill worked on my sliced ear.

"What happened?" I asked.

His voice was calm and soft. "You were in a car wreck."

"I remember being on the road, stumbling around. Someone was on the ground."

Everything started to come back to me. Panicking and scared, I pleaded softly, "Is Janet okay?"

"She'll be fine, just bruised. Chuck wasn't so lucky. The car rolled over him."

"Chuck's dead, isn't he?" I asked as tears started to form.

"Yes, Chuck is gone. Tom has a broken collarbone and will

71

recover."

They wheeled me into the hallway.

My mother was at the hospital to visit my father, who had gone through surgery on his leg two days before. She saw me lying on the gurney, my face covered in mud and blood, and she fainted.

Rumors flew around town about us being in a drunken sex party. The truth was simpler: we had been driving too fast for the road and the vehicle. However, the accident pushed Janet and me further into the outcast cloud. We plunged headlong into our music and each other.

Janet also played the organ for her church each Sunday. This required practice and I would sometimes accompany her to the church during her practice. Most times, we would be alone in the church. One late winter evening we were alone and liberally sprinkled kisses and hugs in between *Rock of Ages* and *The Old Rugged Cross*. We were smooching between hymns when Pastor Politsky strolled around the corner.

He gasped and his jaw descended somewhere near his belt. "What do you two think you're doing?"

"We're practicing," I said.

"Well, you aren't going to practice that type of behavior in this church! Both of you need to go home and think and pray about what you've done here and the trust you violated."

On the steps in the rain, I turned to Janet and we burst into laughter.

"Did you see his face?" I howled.

"I thought he was going to have a fit. He was as red as a beet. I hope he doesn't tell my mom. We'll be up a creek then, Poopsie." She had tagged me with that God-awful pet name.

We walked home enjoying the rain.

On a warm spring Sunday afternoon, we drove out to Plum Creek for a picnic in a grove of sumacs. Janet's father, Speed, let me drive a very nice lime green '54 Chevy convertible that he had for sale. Lying on the soft, sweet grass of the sumac grove, we wondered why it was always so pure and green there. We wondered about many things as we whiled away the sunny day. I never wanted it to end.

During the summer, I got a job working for the local Ford dealer, detailing and washing cars. I was able to buy a very cool one-owner black '41 Ford. I enhanced the paint job with red and yellow flames, red wheels, and moon hubcaps.

The Black Bomb gave us mobility to do more and it provided privacy. Our relationship had become more and more physical. Controlling our passions was a struggle. We worried about not being able to complete high school. They didn't allow pregnant girls in school and we had our hearts set on college.

We decided to cool our relationship and date others with thoughts of renewing our bond at the start of the next summer. It didn't turn out that way. I began dating the woman I eventually married and in the process, I broke Jan's heart.

At our fiftieth reunion, her address and phone number showed up in the class roster. She was living in Northern Idaho and I planned to visit my little brother in Kennewec, Washington. While there, I called her and she was glad to hear from me. We had not talked in all those fifty years. She invited me to visit for a couple of days.

While catching up, we discovered our lives were like a parallel universe: we'd each married three times. We loved sailing, classical guitars, sports cars, and model trains.

I asked her, "Where do you think we would be now if we had stayed together?"

"I think off the coast of Bora Bora in a 40-footer. That's what I would want and I believe you would too."

It was always our tack to sail against the wind.

For two years after that reunion, we continued to get closer. Husker football was important to us as she had played in the University of Nebraska marching band in college. I would call her and we'd talk about the games. I helped her select a new camera, and she knitted sweaters for me. I was calling her more frequently and making plans to visit her in the summer.

That spring, she sent me photos of her new sled and Malamutes she was so proud of there in the Bitterroots.

*William A. Spradley*

I called her two weeks before her fatal heart attack and we talked about my pending visit. Three weeks later, the call from a friend about her passing sent a dagger through my heart.

We had stumbled through life trying to find what we wanted, when what we wanted was each other.

# Visiting Jeary

I hadn't seen him for a year. Since then the stroke and his age had taken a heavy toll on his body and mind. Gerald was my older brother and it hurt to see the shell of this once robust, hard charging, Nebraska farmer, who always seemed to be in perpetual motion.

He sat in the assisted living dining area at Clark Jeary, with his back to me. The room had the appearance of a scene from *One Flew Over the Cuckoo's Nest*. Behind him, a woman rocked back and forth, periodically shouting, "What are we having?"

At the table in front sat another woman who appeared normal, until she brought forth a litany of questions directed at me. "What's the secret? Can you share the secret? Can't you tell me who you are? I don't know you, do I?"

The urge to turn around and run out of the place welled up inside. I had to tell myself, *This is your brother. You have to ignore this to see him.*

Dressed in his ever-present bib overalls – he had tried wearing them to his wedding – he resembled my brother, but something was missing. The quick smile, the sharp sarcastic wit, the infectious laugh, had all been sliced away by the stroke and 87 years of hard work and hard living. Our relationship had been marked with alternates of jokes and arguments. Politics was especially contentious between us, and led to very heated discussions. When our father was around, the atmosphere was like swimming in a vat of poison.

The women in the family shook their heads in disgust and admonished us to change the subject. They never understood how we could argue and shout at one another one minute, then walk outside and look at some new toy one of us had acquired, talking about the fun of it. We all seemed to be able to forget the arrows and rocks we threw.

Gerald was fifteen years older than me, and our brother Carl was born two years before him. They were close but still tolerated me and would take me along when antique hunting at estate sales and running around looking for machinery parts. We would sometimes drive a hundred miles for a good farm sale. During the trip we'd reminisce about the good old days, hunting, cars, our old man, the idiots in Washington. The subjects were varied and hotly contested.

The three of us were true bargain hunters and would have been at home on *American Pickers*. Gerald searched for farm equipment and tools, Carl scouted out antique furniture, and I generally found radios and clocks. We were seldom together, but when we were, this is what we did for entertainment.

Carl and I shared a love of boats and seafood. On return trips from Europe, I'd stop to see him in New York. We would head down to his boatyard, grab some Heinekens and a bucket of steamed clams and crabs, and go for a cruise. The seventeen years difference in our ages melted away when we smelled the fresh salt air of the open sea.

We both loved practical jokes and would often game one of his twin boys or a son-in-law into buying the beer.

Carl's favorite bar on Sheepshead Bay had a dock. They would deliver the beer, charging the boys for bringing it to the boat. We would glance at one another and chuckle about them being such dumb shits. They could have just walked to the bar at the end of the dock and saved ten bucks.

You had to watch your ass around my family. There were no prisoners taken and no mercy given. Carl's passing tore a supersize hole in my soul. He was my hero from the time I could first remember.

At Clark Jeary, I sat with Gerald as he received his lunch. His fork moved agonizingly slowly, and it was an effort to get food to his mouth. He attempted to tell me something, but the words were hanging there somewhere in that formerly razor-sharp mind. I saw the frustration on his face and the pain it brought him. I tried to finish his sentences for him and he would shake his head yes or no, depending on how well I guessed. I could tell that his thought process and recognition still functioned as he would form a smile when the other patients made off-the-wall comments. We exchanged knowing glances as the woman in front of him wandered around and asked bizarre questions of the people near her.

He appeared to be comfortable with his fate. It was impossible to tell for sure, as he wouldn't, or couldn't, talk about it. I had been to visit the year before when his family had auctioned off most of his "toys." He stood in the living room watching while tractors, combines, hay rakes, and harnesses for the horses disappeared out of the barnyard. We left him alone with his thoughts, stoically silent while his dreams and hard work rolled past the window.

I knew what my brother was going through. The year before, I sold my treasured sailboat and Fiat Spider. It isn't the physical part of growing old that hurts, it's the losses and departures that wear you down, the friends and family that pass on before you. It takes a toll.

I visited Clark Jeary Assisted Living one more time before I headed back to St. Louis.

We didn't have much to say to one another. We sat silent for most of an hour with an occasional comment about weather or Husker football. In my family, hugs and "I love you's" were rare. I never received either from my father, and I can count on one hand the times my mother dished out anything close to that.

When I rose up to leave, he grabbed my hand and held on. I probably wouldn't see him again.

All I could think about was how much I loved him. I reached over, gave him a short hug and walked out.

*William A. Spradley*

## Hotel California

Since I was getting away from a bad marriage and a difficult divorce, a move to the Netherlands was my chosen fix. Immersing myself in my career would save me. But after a year of pouring all my effort into work, I was exhausted. A holiday seemed to be the cure. I found a reliable travel agent just off the Langevoorhout in The Hague, where I worked.

"What kind of a holiday are you looking for?"

"I've been looking at flatland and big cities for over a year. I need mountains and fresh air. Maybe some hiking and climbing. Peace and quiet sounds good."

"Austria may be just right for that. There's a small hotel near Fern Lake. An Austrian woman and her American husband run it. It's reasonable with full pension available. Very remote."

"What's the name of this place?"

"Hotel California."

I was reminded of the old Eagles tune. I said, "Oh my, I can check out, but I can never leave? Sounds spooky."

"I assure you, many have recommended this hotel. Good food, comfortable rooms, pleasant owners. It's a little rustic, but sounds like what you're after."

"OK, let's do it."

*****

In early June tourists had yet to swarm over Western Europe. Light misty rain slowed my progress down the German Autobahn and hid the countryside from my view. At times, the rain became heavy. Unable to see the flashing lights of Mercedes and Porsches, I drove with great caution.

Stopping for lunch at a roadside restaurant near

78

Heidelberg and knowing schnitzel and bratwurst would be plentiful in the next two weeks, I ordered a salad. As I lingered a little too long over coffee, the weather took a turn for the worse. Driving rain and strong winds followed me all the way to the Tyrol. I hoped this wasn't a harbinger of what was to come during my stay in Austria.

The Hotel California wasn't difficult to find, because it was only a short distance off the highway near Fern Lake. Arriving in late afternoon, I found it strange to see the name *Hotel California* above the door of a Tyrolean chalet.

A tall, slim man who looked to be in his early thirties greeted me at the desk. "May I help you?"

"Yes, I have a reservation for today."

"Ah, you must be the American from Holland. We have a room with a balcony that overlooks the lake. Does that sound all right?"

"Excellent. By the way, where are you from originally?"

"Born and raised in Ventura, California. Hence the name of my hotel. Met a girl from here when I was an exchange ski instructor, loved the place and her. Never had a desire to go back to the States."

"I know the feeling. I've been living in the Netherlands for the past year. It'll be hard to return to the Midwest."

"Yep. Dinner is served in the dining room at 1830. There's a small bar. Breakfast begins at six and runs until nine. If you want a sack lunch to take while hiking, let us know at dinner and it'll be ready in the morning. Anything else?"

Thinking he had covered it all, I said, "No, that should do it."

Tall with sun-bleached hair, he flashed that friendly Southern California smile, "Enjoy."

*****

The dinner crowd was sparse. Two couples sat together, another couple by themselves, and a stunning flaxen-haired beauty occupied the table next to me reading the *Algemen Dagblad*, a Dutch newspaper. She didn't look up when I sat down.

### William A. Spradley

The schnitzel was delicious as it always is in this part of
Europe. The Austrian wine was new and a bit on the sweet
side. Ordinary, but tasty enough.

After coffee, I headed to the bar and ordered another glass
of the red. I had taken the first sip when the flaxen-haired
beauty eased onto the stool next to me and said, "You know it's
not good for you to drink alone. People will think you're a
drunk."

"I'll drink to that," I said as I turned her way.

"*Garcon*, I will have the same thing he's drinking."

"Where are you from?" I asked. "I detect a Dutch accent."

"I'm from Drenthe. And you?"

"Originally from Evergreen, Colorado. I work in *Den
Haag*, now."

"Do you have a name? Mine's Joni."

"Glen. Pleased to meet you, Joni. So, what are you doing
here?"

"Getting away. From my job. From my family. From
Holland. I just had to get out of there before my head exploded.
Ever had that feeling?"

"A few times. I needed a break from work and the
monotony of the city and the flat landscape. I was raised in the
mountains and I always have to get back to them to feel at
home."

She raised her glass in a salute. "*Prost.*"

I returned the toast. "I'm thinking of hiking up to Fern
Pass tomorrow. What are you doing?"

"Nothing planned. Fern Pass sounds good. You're not
thinking of setting any speed records, are you?"

"No. We can have an easy walk. There's a café at the top.
We should be able to make it in time for lunch, and then back
here for dinner."

"You have everything figured out, don't you?"

"I'm good at organizing; that's my job. Early breakfast?
Say six-thirty?"

"Yep. See you in the morning."

I watched her walk away and couldn't keep my eyes off of

## Interludes & Lunch

the fluid movement of her hips. *Son, you may have hit the jackpot.*

*****

At breakfast, we shared a table and studied the map for trails to Fern Pass. I asked the waiter to make a couple thermoses of coffee for us.

The path began behind the hotel. It was an old Roman road with deep ruts from two thousand years of wagons traversing the Alps. We started out in light mist, but it burned off and warmed up by mid-morning. When we broke for coffee, I asked if she had ever been married.

"Yes. I have, and that's all I will say about it. How about you?"

"That's why I'm in Holland. I needed to start over after it ended."

"You still love her?"

"I don't hate her. I just couldn't understand what happened. I thought I was a good husband. Had no idea she'd been seeing someone for several months. I was too busy to notice."

"Don't beat yourself up. She probably just had a wanderlust. She needed a change."

*****

Larches and spruce trees, with a few maples and oaks, shaded the trail. Mountain bluebells and wild lilies freshened the air with sweet scents. Now and then, Edelweiss peeked out from the rocks. An old Roman bridge, precisely made from local granite, crossed a tumbling river. One arch spanned the waters. A few stones had begun to crumble and the deck of the bridge had deep ruts like the road. Still intact and passable, it added to the history and magic of the area. We treaded lightly over the bridge, enjoying the view up the gorge, where glaciers covered the upper reaches of the mountains. The melt from that ancient ice created rolling cold streams of white water. Postcard quality all the way to the pass.

At lunch, I asked about her taste in music.

"Jazz and blues, also country. I'm not much on pop music.

81

Guess I'm old school."

"Our likes are similar. Do you know that you have the most beautiful pale green eyes?"

"You want something, don't you?"

"Why wouldn't I? You're delightful."

"Don't get carried away. We hardly know one another. I'll say this. You have handsome blue eyes and silky silver hair. A girl could fall for that. I'm not saying *I* would. Some girls would."

"You're direct. I like that."

Blushing, she looked at her watch. "We should start back if we want to eat."

*****

At the bar after dinner, I asked her plans for tomorrow.

"An easy day. Maybe paddle around the lake."

"Sounds good. Want company?"

"You won't sink the boat, will ya?"

I laughed at her easy humor and teasing ways and found myself thinking of her constantly. She had charmed me in a very short time.

During breakfast, she said, "Okay, we'll get a pedal boat this morning. I want to get some sun since it looks like it might be a very nice day. Now don't get too excited, I'm going to put on my bikini."

"You probably shouldn't go out on a boat alone with me then. I might tell you to sin or swim."

She looked at me out of the corner of her eye and shook her head.

I stood on the dock when she came down the path. She dropped her robe, and I nearly fell off the dock. More gorgeous than I imagined, her creamy white skin offset the black bikini. A sailor's dream.

"You know this is going to be d--difficult," I stuttered.

"Why? All we have to do is pedal and steer."

"Sitting next to you in that bikini will test my self-restraint."

"Settle down, young man, or I'll make you walk the

82

plank."

We pedaled around the island in the middle of Fern Lake. It had been the top of a volcanic mountain; a long time ago, the lava had run out the sides of the volcano and with no support, the peak dropped straight down. It reminded me of Crater Lake back home, but on a smaller scale.

The morning went by as we splashed one another and teased until returning to the hotel at noon. We had lunch on the terrace, enjoying the view and one another.

"I want to do some sunbathing and a little reading this afternoon. Do you mind?"

"Do you want company?" I asked.

"Yes, if you can keep your mouth shut." She smiled and blinked coquettishly. I would do anything she wanted.

I lay beside her, watching her breasts swell and recede with each breath she took, while I tried to get interested in Frederick Forsythe. At last, I rolled close to her and kissed her shoulder. She didn't stir. She stayed engrossed in the Dutch romance novel she was reading. My kisses moved to her neck.

She shivered, turned, and said, "If you are going to start something, you better finish it."

I kissed her open mouth and we held each other close. "Want a little afternoon delight?" I asked.

"No, I want a *lot* of afternoon delight."

We spent the rest of the day in her room, under the duvet. She was sensitive and passionate, and when I lay back, she would start me up again.

At six o'clock she said, "I'm famished. I hope we can have a great big beefsteak for dinner. Come on, let's get ready to eat."

That night we lay naked under the duvet. Our lovemaking was slow and tender, and I didn't want it to end. I was falling for her and I hoped that she felt the same about me. We whispered, "I love you" to one another and talked softly about how much we cared.

*****

We had a late breakfast and decided to climb up the

Grosshorn, the mountain next to the hotel. When we reached the halfway point, we were far above the traffic and silence descended on the mountain. You could no longer hear cars, or machinery, or voices, only the clanging of the bells on the goats that roamed this mountain.

And the cuckoo birds. At first, I thought I was hearing someone's clock, but it happened too often. "Do you hear that, Joni?"

"I didn't realize the clocks sounded so much like the birds. I love it. This is such a magical place. I don't want it to end. But it will."

We climbed to the tree line and looked at the snow on the mountaintop and the glacier flowing down the side. The view was spectacular and a marvel to us both.

*****

For the next week, during the days, we alternated climbing and playing by the lake, reading and discussing our books. The nights, we spent together, exploring and learning about our bodies and our taste for love. Never had I fallen that fast and desired so deeply. The last few days came and went far too quickly. I wasn't ready for our time together to end. We held each other the entire night, neither wanting to let go.

At breakfast the last morning, we ate in silence. Not wanting to say goodbye, we lingered over coffee.

"I want to see you when we get back to Holland," I said.

"I haven't been completely honest with you, Glen."

The tears flowed down her cheeks and words came in little gasps. Her shoulders began to shake. "I told you I had been married, and I'm still married. I needed to get away for a while to decide what to do about my feelings. Glen, I love you, but I can't leave my husband."

I couldn't believe my ears. Pain squeezed my heart. She couldn't be saying this, could she?

"You satisfied that wanderlust I described. I'm sorry if I've hurt you. I didn't mean to, but I can't leave Piet. Can you forgive me?"

Holding back the tears, I sat there trying to fathom what

just happened. "Joni, how could you? I love you and I don't want to lose you. Are you sure this is what you want?"

"Yes, I'm sure. I'm sorry I have to do this, but I'm not sorry for having spent these last two weeks with you. You are a wonderful lover and a true gentleman. Best of luck, eh?" She stood up and headed for the checkout desk.

Riveted to my chair, I couldn't move. She walked out the door to her car. I told myself, *You fool; you have to get her back.*

Her BMW pulled out of the parking lot and headed north.

Stunned, I couldn't get my brain to function. Emotions had taken over. By the time reality returned, there was no chance to catch her.

*****

As I drove down out of the mountains, my brain was in a fog. My car was speeding along the Autobahn before my sense of presence returned. Visions of our time together rolled through my head.

I stopped at a rest area on the outskirts of Stuttgart. Standing beside the car, everything came out – breakfast, my anger, and my self-pity. *What did I do wrong? When will the hurting end?*

*William A. Spradley*

## WHEN A MAN LOVES A WOMAN

Her name was Marianne and she was the waitress,
barmaid, cook, and sometimes hotel desk clerk at the Bowling
Centrum/Den Helder Hotel. Forty, divorced, blonde, blue-eyed,
pretty and full of impish humor. She liked to tease and give me
extra attention because I liked it and was good at teasing in
return.

On an extra-blustery and cold early spring day, I decided
to spend some time at the bowling alley bar. When I walked in,
the only customers in the place were a couple bowling in the far
lanes. I headed for the bar and when Marianne saw me, she
smiled and said, "Well, now my day is really complete. No
customers, and the miser walks in."

"There are other places to go, you know."

"You won't because you haven't had your daily dose of
abuse. I know you love that." She was correct. I missed the
barbs and stones that flew in my direction. Drawing me a
*Kleintje*, she asked, "How's it going with the girlfriend?"

"It's not going. It's over."

"What did you do, cheat on her?"

She was trying to get me fired up, but I wasn't biting.
"No, she just wasn't honest. That doesn't work for me. The sad
part is it took me a year to figure it out. How about you? What's
happening in your love life?"

"Mike went back to the States and I haven't heard a thing
from him in three months, so I guess that one is over too."

I chuckled. "We are a sorry pair, aren't we? We learn the
hard way."

"Always."

"Where is everybody today?"

86

"There's a neighborhood festival that a lot of people go to today. They'll be in later, I think." She left to check out the bowlers and the front desk. "Well, it is just us two now." She pulled out the leather cup with the five dice in it. "Want to play horse?"

"Sure."

Handing me the dice cup, she said, "Put some guilders in the jukebox, please."

"I will if you make me one of those pork-on-a-stick thingies.

"A satay? Okay, but don't expect too much."

"You're cooking, so why would I expect much?"

She laughed and stuck out her tongue."You are such a mean man." She headed toward the kitchen.

I yelled after her, "That's what you like about me."

She came back to the bar and rolled the dice in between checking the satay and warming up a spicy peanut sauce. She brought out the satay with the sauce, and we shared it while we played horse. We tired of horse, ate our fill, and started talking about relationships and how they can go sour.

My wallet was lying on the bar and she picked it up and looked through the pictures. "Is this your daughter?"

"Yes, you know that. You met her last year."

"Do you have a picture of your ex-wife?"

"No. Why would I carry her around?"

She was going through all of my pictures and came to one at the bottom of a pile. "This is her, isn't it?" It was an old photo of my ex that I didn't realize was still in the stack. She waved it around and told me, "Ha, I think I'll keep it and show everyone who comes in here."

"Put it back or I'll put your ass in the sink."

"Ha, you aren't man enough."

I got down off the stool and started after her. Running and waving the photo around, she made her break. Catching her before she got to the bowling alley, I picked her up and put her over my shoulder and went back to the bar with her pounding on my back yelling, "Put me down, you beast!"

### William A. Spradley

When we got behind the bar, I set her down not too gently in the sink. She was yelling Dutch obscenities and splashing water at me.

When I let her go, Marianne hopped down from the sink and examined her posterior. "You animal, I have to work the rest of my shift with a wet butt."

"Hey, you shouldn't have teased me."

She looked at me and smiled. "Now you have to pay for that."

"And how would I do that?"

"You must dance with me." She walked to the jukebox and said, "I need guilders." I handed her all the change in my pocket and she punched up Percy Sledge, *When a Man Loves a Woman*. It was her favorite, along with Dr. Hook's *When You're in Love With a Beautiful Woman*.

We danced and held each other close through six cycles of Percy and it was getting very dreamy in the Bowling Centrum. Marianne's Chanel No. 5 was beginning to intoxicate me, and I felt myself falling under her spell. Feeling her body close to mine warmed me through and through. I didn't want it to end.

Wrapped up in one another, we didn't hear the front door open and two men walk into the bar. We were in the middle of a long passionate kiss when I heard, "Is this the Bowling Centrum or the sex-shop?"

It was Hans and Johann, two crazy people who frequented the bar. Johann said, "Boy, oh boy. We'll watch the bar if you want to get a room, Tom."

Marianne and I both turned bright red. She went back behind the bar and I returned to my stool. We looked at one another and smiled.

The bar was filling up with people coming from the festival. It was time to leave.

I would see her at the Bowling Centrum every now and then, and occasionally we would meet in town at the market. Sometimes if she was behind the bar, I would punch up Percy Sledge on the jukebox and we would give each other a knowing smile.

88

*Interludes & Lunch*

Mike came back into her life and I met the love of my life a short time later. We never danced together again. I often wonder what might have been.

*William A. Spradley*

## THEE BIJ TANTE JOSEPHINE
### (Tea with Aunt Josephine)

She was my mother's sister. As long as I can remember, Mom and I had afternoon tea at her house every Friday. A stoutly-built woman, Josephine had the solid look of a farmer's wife. She never married and worked as a nurse all of her life. Despite her demeanor being a bit formal, she loved to laugh and play some sort of trick or joke on me. She served tea proper and genteel. The heirloom Delft blue tea set from the Netherlands gave the impression of having tea with Miss Havisham.

Tante always referred to me as her *kleintje*. She felt that I should learn at least a little of a tongue not my own. *"Wilt U een koek hebben?"* If I wanted a cookie, I had to reply in Dutch including all the courtesies necessary for showing proper respect for elders.

Josephine was a pretty woman with blonde hair that became increasingly whiter as the years went by. When I was the age that the opposite sex began to fascinate me, and women and girls were able to cast spells on me only with their looks, I asked her if she ever had a boyfriend or a husband.

Tante's shoulders slumped, she sighed heavily and a cloud passed over her eyes. She hesitated before she replied. "Ach! I had a boyfriend once. Handsome. And very brave. When you are older, I will tell you our story."

Young women in their late teens and early twenties when World War II ended, mother and Josephine lived through a frightening time. From what I heard and read, their lives were miserable during the war.

"Oh *ja*," my mother told me one day after being pestered

90

to tell me about her youth. "Times were difficult. No food, no fuel for heat, and the Nazis came to our house and took our bicycles and our radio. We tried to hide things but they were very shrewd and ferreted out what you had hidden. Sometimes we ate tulip bulbs. Potatoes seldom made it to our table. We did what we could. Sometimes I rode a bike thirty kilometers all the way from Breezand to Haarlem to try to find vegetables. Meat? Impossible to find. Many nights we went to bed hungry. The soldiers had taken my father away to work in a factory in Germany. We never saw him again. Later, we found out he died when B-17 bombers destroyed the factory. Oh *ja*, it was a very hard time."

Just a few days ago I had been annoyed when I realized we were out of my favorite cereal. I now felt ashamed for being petty and selfish. This was nothing compared to the hardships and disappointments my mother and Josephine had gone through. I lived a very sheltered life.

As a teenager, I became more interested in my mother's life in Holland. History became my passion and I aspired to become a teacher. I needed to know about her life. How could they have coped with the deprivation and terror of war and occupation?

"We had faith the Americans would come save us. We had our faith in God and we worked hard to try to provide enough food for ourselves. People are much tougher and more resilient than they think. My mother sheltered us from some of the troubles, but we knew what was happening and that it might not turn out to our good fortune." My mother paused before continuing. "And so we learned to live with doubt. No carefree teenage years for Josephine and me."

"Well, Mama, I have read about the Dutch underground. Did you know of any people involved in that?"

"Yes, very well. You should ask Tante Josephine. She was very much a part of it and it cost her dearly."

In my high school years, I seldom had time for tea with Tante. Sports and girls kept me busy. Mother passed away unexpectedly during my senior year. Father had a very difficult time with it. The sadness stayed with him until he died of a broken heart soon after I left for college. My only remaining family was Josephine. Though I was rarely able to return home to Omaha, during one of those trips Josephine answered the question I had asked long ago.

She took a few deep breaths, closed her eyes, and sighed. "Oh my, it has been so long since I have talked about that time. It never really goes away, but you put it in a corner so it doesn't weigh too heavy on your mind. Do you have time? It may take me a while to remember."

"I have as much time as it takes. I'd love to hear your story."

Josephine held her breath a bit before she spoke. "Where should I start? Let's see. I met Hank at a friend's party. Handsome, tall, dark hair, and he had a wonderful sense of humor. He attended medical school and had a brilliant mind. I fell for him instantly. Like being struck by lightning."

"Ah, so you did have a boyfriend."

"*Ja,* we were very happy, but because of school, we didn't have much time together. One evening, he told me he was doing his part to fight the Nazis. I asked what he meant by that, and he made me promise not to tell anyone about his involvement. He worked for the underground."

Again, she took a deep breath before continuing.

"He was a member of a chain of people who supplied information to saboteurs so they would know when to strike. He relayed information from a contact in Den Helder to another contact in Alkmaar. He was very brave and it made me love him even more. I asked if I could help in any way. He didn't want me to get involved."

Josephine hesitated. I could tell it was still a very emotional experience for her. Her eyes began to water and her hands trembled.

She poured more tea and then continued. "One night he told me they needed to change messengers so the Nazis wouldn't catch on to the pattern of movement. I loved him and would do anything he asked. For over a year, I carried

92

messages for the underground from Den Helder to Alkmaar."

Josephine's voice came in short bursts, while she sighed deeply in between each sentence. "It was 1945 and very near the end of the war when soldiers broke into Hank's apartment while we were there. They grabbed him and one of them pointed a Luger at his head. A soldier told me I should tell them about his activities or they would shoot him. I became hysterical, but Hank told them, 'She knows nothing and neither do I.' One of them grabbed me and tore my blouse open and told Hank they would rape me if he didn't tell about his contacts."

Her tears flowed, and I put my arm around her. "You don't have to tell me if it is too difficult, Tante."

"No, I want to tell you. You should know."

She dried her tears and began again. "Hank swore at them, calling them *Duit's Varken,* German pigs. The soldier with the Luger struck Hank with the barrel of the pistol. Again, he pointed the gun at Hank's head and told me to tell them what I knew. When I started to talk, Hank glared at me and said, 'She knows nothing. She won't tell you anything because she has nothing to tell.' The soldier pulled the trigger and Hank's blood splattered on the wall. I still see it in my nightmares."

Exhausted, she sat there silent for a few minutes. "They let me go, and told me they would be watching all the time. I never delivered another message."

"Tante Josephine, I can't imagine going through something so horrific."

"I never found anyone like my Hank again, and that is why I never married. I could not put that burden on someone else."

I didn't get a chance to see her again until my wedding. She was happy I'd found someone to share my life. After I was married, it slowly came to me why she had not wanted to burden someone with her sadness and pain.

A few years later, I was in Omaha and brought my son Hank to have tea with Josephine.

*William A. Spradley*

"*Ach wat a mooi kleintje*," she cooed when she saw him. She thought him a handsome boy.

The years had taken their toll on her. Her beautiful blonde hair was now snow white. Her weathered hands trembled when she poured the tea.

It would be the last time I had *thee bij tante Josephine.*

## ALONG CAME YOU

A Mexican cutie with dancing dark eyes and midnight black hair, Milagros kept me mesmerized from the first time she poured a glass of *Take Me*. She tended the evening bar at the Whale's Tail. Watching her work became my evening amusement.

Sent to fix a system problem, I ferreted out the defect, and then passed the time waiting for replacement parts. They could show up any day, so I hung around Oxnard sailing in the morning, lounging by the pool in the afternoon, having cocktail time and the excellent grilled swordfish dinner.

"Saw you out on the water this morning, gringo." She enjoyed harassing and drawing laughter from me. "Your sails were flapping and you were spilling your beer."

"Better my sails flapping than something else."

"Ha, I don't think that would flap, just droop, *sabe*?"

"What did I do for torment before you came along?"

"Maybe *su esposa*?"

That one hurt. "Nah, she adored me."

"So where is this adoring woman now?"

"She left me for a Mexican."

"That is hilarious." Torment was her game.

"I failed to see the humor at the time."

Leaning over to look me in the eye, she said, "It's hilarious because my husband left me for a blonde. A gringo bimbo."

"Boy, we are a couple losers, aren't we?"

"Speak for yourself. I got his Porsche Boxster and his house. The bimbo has to support him now."

"Ouch! You are one mean *chica*. Remind me to never

marry you."

Milagros grinned and left to serve someone else.

Nursing my Corona and reflecting on her flippant attitude, I thought, *She is a fun woman.* The dinner crowd was beginning to filter in and her workload pushed her into speed bartending mode. Time to drop the tip and head for the dining room and the early bird special.

After dinner, I headed to the bar and found it quiet with only an older couple having their coffee and cognac.

"Ay, you came back for more?"

"Yeah, I'm a bloody masochist."

She poured my beer and slid it down the bar, "Very *tranquilo* this evening. I like more action."

"Sure you do," I chuckled. "Would you like to go sailing? I need some ballast."

"You need a bigger boat, sailor. Size matters, *sabe?* I'm off tomorrow if you think you can handle a little salsa."

"Oh, yeah. How about nine-ish in the lobby of the Casa Serena?"

"I'll be there."

She surprised me. I didn't think she had any interest in me other than as a customer.

In the morning, I reserved a Catalina 22. The 22-footer is a reliable craft we could take out to the open sea and have room to be comfortable. The local grocery provided beer and snacks. Milagros strolled into the lobby at 9:10.

"I said nine-ish, not noon," I called to her as she walked in the door.

"Keep your pants on, gringo, we have all day."

While we headed to the marina, she talked about her rough night. "Bartending is killing me, I need a real job."

"Yeah, yeah, you won't quit. It's easy money."

"Oh and putting up with drunks like you is easy?"

"You like it, you know you do. You like me or we wouldn't be here now, would we?" I wasn't going to let her off without some teasing.

"No, I like your big boat, *sabe?*"

96

*Interludes & Lunch*

"Uh-huh." We grabbed some ice at the marina store and boarded the *María*.

"What, no champagne and caviar?" She tried to look disappointed.

"Well, if I had a date with a blonde bimbo, I might have champagne, but since I'm out with a wild Mexican woman, it's Corona and chorizo."

Milagros laughed, punched my arm and said, "You are one loco guy, amigo. I like crazy people."

The sailing across the harbor and out to the Pacific and the Channel Islands was easy. It was a pleasant southern California day with ten-knot breezes and lazy one-foot swells. We cruised between the islands and the Ventura shoreline for most of the morning.

Milagros told me of her parents who picked lettuce and tomatoes in the truck farms of the valley and of the five brothers and sisters she grew up with. I talked about growing up on a Midwestern farm and the joys of pheasant hunting. Although we came from different backgrounds, there were many shared interests. It seemed incongruous to our normal teasing conversations. We were nearly serious.

When the mist and cold afternoon winds arrived at two o'clock as is normal, it was an opportune time to head back toward Oxnard harbor. At five in the afternoon, *María* docked at the marina.

"If you come home with me I'll fix you the best burritos you have ever eaten."

"How can I resist that offer?"

The burritos were divine. Milagos had her own garden where she grew jalapeno and habanera peppers. Everything was fresh, straight from her garden.

The evening passed talking on her patio and drinking Sonoma wines. I didn't make it back to my room at the Casa Serena that night. Both sweet and passionate, Milagros was a delightful companion. She spoke Spanish to me all night, the language of love titillating my senses.

The needed part for the system problem arrived the next

morning. After some testing and tweaking, I declared the problem solved. It was time to head home.

That afternoon I strolled into the Whale's Tail. Milagros was behind the bar and blew me a kiss.

"Ay, you are early. No sailing?"

"No, the new part was waiting for me when I came in and I completed the certification. I have a morning flight back home."

"Oh. I'm off at six. Want to get some dinner?" It was the first time I noticed any trace of melancholy in her voice.

At Charley Brown's we whiled away the evening until time to go our separate ways.

"I'll miss you, gringo. You are a fun guy, *sabe?*"

"I'll miss you too, *chica.*" There was a pain in my chest where breath had been. *Why was this hurting so much?*

Over Kansas, thunderstorms buffeted the 757. It was a miserable flight. All I could think of was midnight hair, dancing dark eyes, and blue water.

# TEA AT TWO

They met at precisely two o'clock every Saturday afternoon at *Le Petit Coin Salon de Thé* in old town Geneva. The window table was their first choice. Normally, chai was their starter; then they moved on to Alsatian wine, laptops in front of them, typing, laughing, and sipping their *Gewurztraminer*. He could tell the two were American by their style of dress, although it wasn't as easy to spot Yankees in Europe as it had been twenty years before. Nowadays Europeans dressed like Americans, while some Americans preferred to dress like Europeans.

He had noticed them each Saturday for the last four weeks, and his curiosity piqued. As he eavesdropped on their conversations, sometimes he struggled to keep from laughing aloud.

An engineer who worked in several different western European countries, he had taken early retirement. Switzerland's mountain paradise was a natural choice for a hideaway. Deciding to pick up a hobby he had wanted to pursue as a career, he wrote short stories and adventure novels.

The fourth Saturday they parked themselves by the window was a pleasant sunny fall day, and he heard the fair-skinned one mention it would be nice to be outside on a day like this. Afternoons near Lac Léman often brought afternoon showers. The dark-haired beauty got up from the table and headed his direction. When she got close, he glanced from his journal and smiled at her. She smiled back and asked, "I see you have a Moleskine journal. Are you a writer?"

"I'm trying, but without much success." He had sold a couple of short stories, but the blockbuster novel seemed far off. "Are you two writers? I see you here each Saturday."

### William A. Spradley

"We're school teachers at the International School of Geneva. However, we're both struggling novelists at heart. We meet here on Saturdays to critique one another's work, exchange ideas, and drink wine. Would you like to join us?"

"You gals seem pretty high-tech for me. I just use a pencil and a journal, but I'd like to join you. Do you mind?"

"Of course not. We've noticed you. You seem very quiet, so we won't mind at all. My name is Raquel, and my friend's name is Desiree."

"I'm Devon. Are you sure you want someone old and slow at your table?"

Raquel winked. "I think you'll fit right in."

He thought, *Do I want to keep my peace and solitude or do I want some younger contact to help brighten up my stories? What do I have to lose?* He walked over to their table and said, "Hi, I'm Devon. You're Desiree, I assume?"

"We've been trying to figure out if you are just a kindly elder gentleman or a lecherous, dirty old man." She laughed.

He liked her direct yet comic approach. "Well, sweetheart, I'm a little of both; ogling like a lecher and observing like a gentleman. I try to imagine what is going on inside people's heads."

Desiree smiled. "Oh, boy, if you knew what went on inside our heads, you would be blushing right now."

Devon chuckled. "I doubt if you could be thinking of something that would make me blush. I've seen and heard most everything." He pulled up a chair to the rattan table and made himself comfortable. "What sort of writing do you do?"

"Desiree sees dead people, so she writes paranormal stories, and I write mostly romances where somebody is killed. Sometimes I get hungry and have to write about food, and then maybe someone falls asleep and drowns in their soup. It's not easy finding ways to kill your lover."

Devon was quick to answer. "There must be fifty ways at least."

"He could slip out the back, Jack," Desireé said. "Or miss the bus – goodbye, Gus."

100

*Interludes & Lunch*

"Does wine make you girls goofy or is it normal for both of you?"

"Normal? Why would we be normal? We're writers. Writers are either drunks or suicidal, and we plan on being around for a while," Raquel explained.

He squinted from one to the other and said, "I'll drink to that. Cheers."

\*\*\*\*\*

Their conversations varied from Saturday to Saturday, depending on what caught their attention that week. Sharing their stories was always the main topic.

One Saturday Raquel asked, "Were you ever married?"

He paused, trying to decide how to answer. "Yes, I had a wife and three children. The children are grown and scattered around the U.S. My wife was killed in a climbing accident here in Switzerland. I've been single since then."

"How terrible," Desireé said. "How long ago was that?"

"Fifteen years."

Raquel added, "Devon, you poor thing."

"You learn to cope, but you never forget. I think of her every day, still. I've written about it a time or two."

The two women pushed the old man to relate his experiences from when he traveled and during his war years. His life produced a series of highs and lows. He had been a Navy Phantom pilot during Vietnam, two MIG kills to his credit, but then he was shot down by flak and captured. Five years in the Hanoi Hilton left his body generously scarred. Waiting for him at home, his wife struggled with loneliness, uncertainty, and the burden of raising three young children. He retired from the service and worked for an aerospace company until time to retire again.

In his early years as an engineer, he had been assigned to work in Switzerland. His wife and he liked to ski and climb. During a climb on the Eiger, she fell and he shattered his leg trying to save her. His failure to prevent her death weighed heavy on his mind.

\*\*\*\*\*

*William A. Spradley*

The weeks went by and the three of them continued to meet through the winter. They became close friends and shared their free time together. They spent Christmas holidays together. Devon traveled with them to Chamonix for a little skiing. He could no longer ski but enjoyed sitting at the mountaintop restaurant's terrace, drinking coffee and schnapps. The two women plied the slopes while he wrote in his journal.

Spring brought them outside and on sunny days, they would sit at the sidewalk tables enjoying the fresh alpine air. The two young women were nearing the end of their contracts and would be transferring back to the United States in the summer.

One pleasant day, he looked at them and said, "You know I will really miss you girls when you head back to the States?"

"Awe, we'll miss you too, Devon. You have been like a father to us," Raquel said, her eyes on the verge of tears.

*****

Devon became quieter and not as quick with a laugh. He would often stare for minutes at a time and his jokes were rare. A light had dimmed.

The first Saturday in May, Raquel and Desireé arrived at La Petite Coin and found Devon's chair unoccupied. Normally, he would be there in a corner when the antique Swiss clock chimed two.

After half an hour, Desiree was worried. "I hope something hasn't happened to him. He's always on time, and he would have called if he wasn't going to be here. I think we should check on him."

They crossed the street to Devon's apartment. There was no answer when Raquel knocked. She tried the handle and the door opened. He was sitting by the window with his chin on his chest. His precious journal had fallen to the floor along with a broken pencil. When she picked up the journal, it was open to a page where the title to a new story was written in number 2 lead – *"Tea at Two."*

102

# IT STARTED WITH A WHISPER

In a packed commodity-trading seminar at the Marriot Hotel in Newport, Rhode Island, a black suit on the podium droned on, extolling the virtues of soybean and wheat futures. Heads drooped, then jerked up to attention, giving the appearance of a convention of St. Vitus Dance sufferers.

When the subject rolled over to pork bellies, she leaned toward the suit next to her and whispered, "Want to get away?"

He turned, smiled and said, "I thought you'd never ask."

"I'll meet you in the lobby."

Near the hotel entrance, he said, "I'm thinking about the Black Pearl Clam House."

"Sounds divine," she cooed.

"My name's Desmond. Just call me Desi."

"Ha," she laughed. "Mine's Lucy. Isn't that crazy?"

"Yeah, Lucy, looks like you got some 'splainin' to do."

*****

At a table on the deck at the Black Pearl, they watched as sailboats cruised by and excursion craft plied the bay. A warm sunny day with a mild breeze made it a perfect afternoon.

"Will you get in trouble for missing the training?" he asked.

"I don't care if I do. My boss is such a creep. I don't think he knows what I look like; he's only noticed my boobs."

"That's funny. I noticed your pale blue eyes and your a…. Well you know, your a… hair." Her hair was nearly white, short and teased; she looked like Meg Ryan in *You've Got Mail.*

"Ha, you're squirming. It doesn't bother me. At least you noticed my eyes."

"You're a pretty woman. Not one-dimensional at all. Are you married or attached?"

"No, I'm a widow. My husband had a heart attack and died while we were having sex. He was a large man and fell on top of me. I had a hard time reaching the phone to call 911. He was sort of 'dead weight,' I guess."

"Good that you can talk about it. My wife was shot by a jealous boyfriend."

"Really?"

"Well, it was actually her boyfriend's boyfriend. Kind of a triangle gone bad. He pumped them full of lead with a .44, and then turned it on himself."

"How dreadful."

"Not really. We were in the process of a divorce. The boyfriend saved my house, my 911 Carrera, and my 401K. Things have a way of evening out."

"Well, we certainly have a lot in common."

Sipping a second glass of Chardonnay, she looked out on the bay and remarked, "The sails are so white and so peaceful. Looks like a pleasant way to spend the day."

"Have you ever been sailing?" he inquired.

"No, but I'd love to try it."

"I have a friend here in town who has a Pearson 32. I could probably use it for the afternoon. You interested?"

"I thought you'd never ask," she whispered.

"Hey, Larry," he said into his cell phone. "Okay to use your boat this afternoon? Thanks, buddy. I'll leave some beer in the reefer."

Turning to Lucy he said. "It's all set. Do you have other clothes? We'll drop by the hotel on the way to Narragansett Yacht Club. I'll grab some Sam Adams and some cheese and sausage and we're on our way to paradise."

*****

"Just drop the lines on the dock and we'll be underway. Mind the boom and the moving lines."

The ten-knot breeze made for a pleasant cruise. A

natural-born sailor, she quickly adapted to crewing. Tacking up
the channel towards Long Island Sound and Block Island
proved exhilarating. Lucy, charmed by the sea, the sails and
Desi's commanding nature, smiled non-stop.

They anchored near Conanicut Island for a beer and
snack break. Conversation flowed between them like they'd
known each other all their lives. A peaceful scene to end the
day.

She leaned against him, listening to Jimmie Buffet, when
he asked, "Would you like to *really* get away?"

"What do you mean?"

"I mean like drop out and cruise from here to eternity. I
could sell my stuff and take my 401K and the life insurance
money from my wife's policy and we could circle the globe for
quite some time. I've been looking for someone like you to
complete the dream."

"I have a ton of insurance money and a house that's paid
for. I believe we could live like this forever." Her eyes danced at
the prospect of an idyllic life. No worries, no responsibilities.
"Count me in."

"Okay, I'm thinking a 42-footer. Something the two of us
can handle, but still big enough to be comfortable. We'll divest
ourselves of all the superfluous stuff. We can buy a boat in
Annapolis, cruise down the Intercoastal Waterway, and head
for the Virgin Islands. From then on, it's wherever our fancy
takes us. The Costa del Sol, the French Riviera, Bora Bora. We
have no boundaries."

"Fantastic, I can tell the creep to take his pork bellies and
put 'em where the sun don't shine."

*****

*Escape* lay moored in the center of Little Harbor in Jost
Van Dyke, British Virgin Islands. A gentle breeze blew the
sweet scent of hibiscus and frangipani across the deck. Desi sat
in the cockpit watching the sun go down over St. Thomas. It
had been a day spent snorkeling at Sandy Split, but now it was
time to relax.

Lucy handed up a piña colada from the cabin. "Time to splice the main brace," she called.

"How about lobster and creole potatoes at Sidney's Peace and Love. Will that do?"

She answered, "Works for me." She sat down beside him.

He put his arm around her shoulder. "I wonder where we'd be if I hadn't told my wife's boyfriend's boyfriend where they were hiding out. Selling orange pulp futures, I guess."

"Yeah, I know. I'd probably still be studying pork bellies if I hadn't put those nitro tablets in John's beer before he took his little blue pill." She smiled. "Dinner?"

"I'll get the dinghy."

## ACKNOWLEDGEMENTS

Several good friends made this book possible. It required the alignment of stars and planets, lots of wine, travel, and time spent on barstools.

First, I will be eternally grateful to my dear friend, Sarah Spence. One night sitting in a restaurant, Sarah looked at me with that winsome smile and told me I should be a writer. I made what I considered a clever remark and she said, "No, I mean it. Find a writers workshop. They can help." Usually I don't take anyone's advice, but I had wanted to become a writer when a teenager. It was the nudge needed.

I found Saturday Writers and they nurtured me into becoming an author. The leaders of that group, Jennifer Hasheider and Rebeca Wise, took me under their collective wings and gave the editing help I required. They always pushed me to improve. Thanks to them, these stories took flight. They're also great wine-drinking partners.

I have to thank my muse and inspiration, Rhonda Farren. She could inspire a dead man to get up and dance. She's in a number of these stories and made them contest winners. Another part of my inspiration, Janice Nolan, provided me with great story material and characters. The evenings I spend with those two fill me with laughter and joy.

It isn't often you get to work with one of your offspring and create something together. My daughter Danielle Spradley is an extremely talented artist. She knew what would add the whimsical touch to the cover of this piece. Being able to work with her warms my heart. Thanks for helping, Danielle, your woodcut cover is beautiful.

A big thank you goes out to my fellow members of Coffee and Critique. Their honesty and encouragement helped turn these stories into pieces of literature.

I have to thank my five children, Kelly, Bill, Juanita, Danielle and Stephan, who tolerated my stories and the embarrassment I caused. I'm sure they thought Alzheimer's had taken control and sent me around the bend.

I have always been a lucky man. Once again, I was fortunate to meet Leigh Michaels, who saw something in me and my stories and took a chance on a raw novice writer. Leigh is a patient and light-handed editor and publisher. Thank you, Leigh, for teaching me the art of writing. I am indeed a lucky man.

# About the Author

William Spradley, a native of Southeastern Nebraska, has spent most of his life traveling the U.S and around the world. In nine years of naval service he cruised the Far East, the Mediterranean, and the Caribbean, and was stationed in several locations around the United States. His employment by a major Aerospace company took him to further travels in Europe, the Middle East and the Far East. He has lived in Spain, the Netherlands, Switzerland and Scotland. Travel has provided the experience on which to base his stories.

A member of Saturday Writers and host of the Saturday Writers Works-in-Progress critique group, he is also a member of Coffee and Critique, a highly regarded weekly support group for prose writers. He has won two First Place awards and two Honorable Mentions for Saturday Writers Short Story contests.

When he isn't writing, you'll find him playing with model trains or guitars, or teasing the horde of grandchildren and great-grandchildren who call him grandpa. Often, he spends time sitting on the terrace of some winery. More often, he is having lunch with friends or at the helm of a sailboat. He now lives in St. Peters, MO.

# OTHER BOOKS FROM PBL LIMITED

Maple Street Stories – Bob Nandell
Engraved in the Bark – Elizabeth Ridge
Evasive Dreams – Loren N. Horton
Inklings – Jo'An Hennen
Offerings & Sacrifices – Bob Nandell
Rare Gifts than Gold – Loren N. Norton
Alligator Blues and other poems – Kaitlyn Daniels
"Watch the Cow, Tillie!" – Dale Schwartz
1904 St. Louis World's Fair – Lemberger / Michaels
Focus on Photos – Michael W. Lemberger
One Man's Vision – Michael W. Lemberger
Buxton Roots – Lee Ann Simmers Dickey
Buxton Branches – Lee Ann Simmers Dickey
Before Buxton – Lee Ann Simmers Dickey
Aviation – Lemberger / Michaels

PBL Limited is a small commercial publisher specializing in local history and niche-market books. For more information about these and other publications, or about the publisher, visit www.pbllimited.com

www.ingramcontent.com/pod-product-compliance
Lightning Source LLC
Chambersburg PA
CBHW060650260626
47161CB00008B/3081